Cascades

General Editor: Geoff Fox

The Fox in Winter

The Fox in Winter

John Branfield

CollinsEducational

An imprint of HarperCollins*Publishers*

The author wishes to acknowledge the assistance of the
Arts Council of Great Britain.

ISBN 0 00 330000 5

First published by Victor Gollancz Ltd, 1980
Published in *Cascades* in 1983 by Collins Educational
Reprinted 1985, 1987 twice, 1988, 1989, 1991
Printed and bound in Great Britain
by Martins of Berwick

For Pep again

One

The first of the phone calls came when Frances was alone in the house, doing her homework.

"Stennack-four-oh-double-four-who's-speaking-please?" she said all in one breath, using the formula she had adopted as a young child, when she was always taking phone messages for her mother and not getting the name of the caller. She thought it now sounded rather childish, and when she remembered she would give the exchange and number only, but somehow the whole expression kept slipping out. She immediately regretted it, and as no one spoke at the other end of the line she repeated "Stennack four-oh-double-four" more as she would like it to sound.

There was no reply. It was not a call from a public phone-box, as there had been no continuous pips. The line was still alive and she could hear someone breathing, very heavily.

It's an anonymous caller, she thought.

She wondered if someone was playing a joke on her; and yet at the same time she felt quite frightened, being on her own in the house and not knowing when her mother would return.

"What do you want?" she asked sharply.

The heavy breathing turned into the very deliberate voice of an old man not much used to speaking on the phone. "Is that the nurse?" he asked.

"She's not here," Frances answered.

"Is that the nurse?" he repeated.

She realised that he was deaf. "She hasn't come back from work yet," she said loudly. "Can I take a message?"

But the old man seemed to hum and haw, and then the line went dead. And she had not even taken his name. "Why didn't you ask him?" Nancy would say crossly. She hated to know that someone was trying to get in touch with her and not know who it was, even if it was about something quite trivial.

I didn't have a chance, thought Frances. She probably would not mention the call. Nevertheless, she glanced at the clock on the kitchen mantelshelf, and noted that it was ten past seven.

Sometimes Frances felt like rebelling against answering the phone. The whole point of her life so far, from as early as she could remember, seemed to be to provide an answering service for her mother. Telephone calls could never be as important as all that; if it really mattered the caller would ring again. Once or twice she would let the phone ring on and on, but she always picked it up before it stopped.

One day she would refuse to answer; she would go on reading. "The phone rang but I didn't bother to answer it," she would say. She could imagine nothing that would make her mother more furious.

It rang again twice, in quick succession. The first call was from the matron of a private nursing home, who asked if the nurse could ring her back as soon as she came in.

"I'll pass the message on," said Frances, like an efficient secretary.

She could hear her mother's response. "I'm not ringing her, let her ring me! She only wants to cadge some equipment from the Health Service."

She had hardly replaced the receiver before it rang once more. This time it was Rosemary, the other district nurse for the village and the surrounding countryside. She wanted to go through the list of patients and share out the work for the next day.

"Mum's not home yet," said Frances.

"Not home yet!" exclaimed Rosemary. "I hope she's not stuck in the snow." It had been Rosemary's day off duty. "I'm going out for the evening and won't be back until late. Tell your mum I'll ring her in the morning, and we'll settle the work then. Bye."

Frances wrote down the message on the pad beside the telephone.

Her mother rang at half past seven.

"Hullo, Fran dear!" Nancy's voice was always very young and cheerful on the phone. "Any messages for me?"

"Why are you so late?" She meant it to sound like a concerned enquiry, but it came out more like a complaint. "What's happened?"

"Oh, I've been held up a bit at Mrs Richards's. I shall be back in an hour or so. I wondered if the surgery had rung up."

"No."

"Any calls?"

"About twenty-seven."

"Seriously."

"One or two, nothing important. Rosemary is going out and will ring in the morning. The matron wants you to ring her *as soon as you come home*." Fran played up to her mother's image of the matron.

"Bugger the matron!" said her mum.

"Well, she didn't put it quite like that," said Fran.

"Are you all right, love?" asked Nancy. "Have you found something to eat? Are you getting on with your homework?"

Frances assured her mother that she was quite all right.

★

The next call came at ten to eight. She knew at once that it was the old man again. There was the same slow drawing in of breath followed by its noisy expulsion.

"Will you give me your name?" she asked.

"Is that the nurse?" the voice demanded.

"What is your name?"

"This is Mr Treloar . . . I didn't want to trouble you, but . . ." He seemed unable to continue.

Frances felt a sense of panic. She wished her mother had been there to take the call, she would have known exactly what to do. Fran felt a surge of pity for the old man, his voice was so pathetic. And yet at the same time she felt revulsion too. She did not like old people and pain and emotion. She wanted to keep it away from herself, at a distance. And at the same time she felt sorry for him, this dignified old voice, so broken and despairing.

"You see . . . my wife has fallen down . . ." he continued.

"You must phone the doctor," she said almost coldly.

"I don't like to disturb him."

"That's what he's there for."

"And the nurses are always so good . . . I thought if she could have a look . . ."

"Phone the doctor," enunciated Frances very clearly.

"Is the nurse there?"

"No, you must phone the doctor."

She put the receiver down. The last time she had taken a message of despair, and written it all down, her mother had come home and said, "Oh not him again! He's a real hypochondriac! Why didn't he ring one of his daughters? There are two living on the same estate. And he's got neighbours, hasn't he? I wish I'd answered the phone, I'd have given him a good telling off!"

It was difficult to tell which were genuine. Perhaps they all were. But if the old man's wife had fallen down, then she needed help. At least Fran had covered herself by telling him to call the doctor.

People were always speaking to her on the phone as though she was her mother. She was always being given personal details, particularly about the state of people's bowels. She tried to stop them, but they seemed to have worked themselves up to the point of speaking, and once they were through, it made no difference whether they were talking to the nurse or a recording machine or the nurse's daughter. If they had made up their mind to describe how they felt—"I feel as though cold water is flowing all over my body just under my skin"—then they were compelled to continue.

She went on with her homework, which she finished without further interruption at nine o'clock. Her mother had still not come back. She packed up her books on the kitchen table and put things ready for the next day. She wondered whether to watch television, but it was in the other room, where there was no fire. She could switch on the electric heater, but it seemed cold and cheerless in there. She sat close to the kitchen stove.

It was a cheerless house altogether. The ceilings were high, the windows ill-fitting and draughty. But Nancy was not very concerned. She had no interest in decorating or do-it-yourself. She did not even try to get the health authority to make repairs or repaint the rooms.

"Why don't you do it?" she would say, if Fran suggested redecorating the kitchen or living room.

They had lived there as long as Fran could remember, though in the past they had shared it with a whole succession of other mothers and their children. She often thought about the sort of house that she would like to live in.

She jumped when the phone rang. This time it was the doctor, and he recognised her voice.

"Hullo, Doctor Turner here. Is the Enema Queen at home?"

She did not think he was funny. "I don't know who you mean," she said icily.

"I mean the good lady of the house."

"She hasn't come back yet."

"Good grief! What's she doing?"

"She rang at half past seven to say she was with Mrs Richards and she'd be about another hour."

"She'll be delighted to hear this! So break it to her gently. Will you ask her to go and see a Mrs Treloar at Penhallow Farm? Just clean her up, get her to bed and make her comfortable. Have you got that?"

Fran repeated the name and address.

"Tell her I'd give her a hand, only I've got another call. Okay?"

"Right."

"Bye, Fran."

She was annoyed that the use of her Christian name pleased her. She did not have a high opinion of Doctor Turner, who had taken the place of the old village doctor. He was fortyish and from up-country, and was always in a rush. He seemed to be acting the part of the busy practitioner.

It was not long before she heard a car drive up to the garage. A moment later her mother was pushing hard at the kitchen door, which always jammed in winter, and then she burst into the room.

"Hullo, love, are you all right?"

She pulled off her district nurse's hat, a navy-blue beret with a sort of wing on one side, and shook free her blonde hair. Her blue coat was dotted with flakes of snow, rapidly turning into drops of moisture, and she took this off too, and stood in front of the stove. She had a stiff white apron pinned to her blue dress. There was a row of pens and a thermometer in her breast pocket, and a nurse's watch pinned to the front.

"Poor old Amy Richards!" she said. "She's not going to last much longer."

Fran made a sort of strangled noise.

"What's the matter?" asked Nancy sharply.

"Nothing."

"What did you make that noise for?"

"I don't know," said Fran. "You always come in and say something like that."

"Like what?"

"'Poor old Amy Richards's not going to last much longer.'"

"Well, she's not."

Her mother looked tired. "Do you want something to eat?" Fran asked.

"No, I'll have a drink."

She emptied her pockets and put the contents by the side of the phone, then drew up one of the kitchen chairs to the stove.

"What's the matter with Amy Richards?" asked Fran, as she filled the kettle.

"When I got there this morning she was in agony. I said to her husband, 'Why didn't you call the doctor?' He's on the phone, but they're all the same, they never want to trouble the doctor. He'd rather let his poor little wife suffer. Oh, it makes me so cross!

"And then when I took down her dressing I could have died! The wound had spread to her throat, she was pouring pus everywhere. The stench was terrible."

Fran winced. Nancy's descriptions were very graphic. She never seemed to think that Fran might not want to hear them. It was not as though she was talking to her, it was more a need to go over the experiences of the day in order to be able to live with them. She had to tell someone.

"I got two largactil into her, and cleaned it up as well as I could. You could look down into the wound and see

13

the veins throbbing. She hadn't felt any pain at all before, so she hadn't had many drugs, but now she was very distressed. I went to the surgery and told Doctor Turner, but he just said give her more largactil. Eventually I persuaded him to come out and see her. He gave me some diamorphine and I gave her an injection, but it took ages for it to have any effect. She begged me not to leave her, but I had some other patients to go to."

It reminded Fran that Doctor Turner had left a message for her mother, but she waited before telling her.

"When I went back she was sleeping soundly. She looked very peaceful. She'd got her colour back. I thought I'd give her another injection in the evening to take her through the night, but just before you came home I had a phone call from Jacky to say that Amy was very bad.

"When I got out of the car I could hear all the radios and televisions on the estate turned up loud. They were trying to drown the noise that Amy was making. It was terrible. She had never complained all those months. She had always been such a good woman, always helping the old folk. Even in her bedroom you could hear the radio next door blaring out.

"I gave her a suppository, I wanted to keep the injection for later. Jacky asked how long it would be. He seemed to be thinking of weeks. I told him it could only be two or three days now. I assured him we'd keep her well sedated. She'd come round from time to time and she'd know him and they'd be able to talk. She'd just slip away easily. It could be tonight, I hope so really.

"Anyway, I drummed it into him that if anything happens in the night, to ring the doctor and not me!"

She began to unpin her white apron.

"The doctor rang," said Fran. "He's left a message for you."

"What was it?"

"He wants you to go to a Mrs Treloar at Penhallow Farm."

"Oh no!" moaned Nancy. "That's all I need! I'm not going down to Penhallow on my own, not in the dark."

"Why not?"

"I went there in the daytime once. It's down a long track and then you have to leave the car because the hedges have grown in and push your way between brambles and gorse until you get to the farm, all on its own in a valley. I'm not easily scared, but I'm not doing that."

She moved towards the telephone. "I'll ask Rosemary to come."

"I told you, she's gone out for the evening. She's going to ring tomorrow morning."

"Blast!" She turned and looked at Fran. "Then you'll have to come with me," she said.

It was snowing heavily when they went out to the car, and the windscreen was already covered.

"Have you got your boots?" shouted Nancy, and Frances went through the headlights of the car to fetch them from the garage. The snow was driving across the light.

Nancy reversed the car into the road through the permanently open gates, leaving fresh tyre tracks in the covering of snow. Fran ran round and got into the passenger seat. She huddled into her coat, waiting for the car to warm up.

The wipers cleared two fan-shaped spaces on the windscreen, and Nancy sat well forward, holding the wheel tight and peering out into the darkness.

"I hate the snow!" she said.

Fran was enjoying the sense of drama, of leaving the house and driving out into the cold night on a mission of mercy. She had a picture of St Bernard dogs, barrels of brandy attached to their collars, walking out into the snows of a mountain pass. "Perhaps we shall get snowed-in!" she said.

"Don't say that! I don't want to walk home in the middle of the night."

"It would be fun."

"It's no fun for the old people. They get very anxious when it's snowing."

"It looks lovely," said Fran. The road ahead of them was all white, and the cottages of the village street were transformed with white roofs and thick white window-sills. There were no people about and no other cars were on the roads.

"I hope I can get out in the morning. I shall have to walk round if I can't. I must get to Amy Richards fairly early. And I've one diabetic injection which can't wait."

"Couldn't she do her own?"

"She's blind, she can't see how much insulin she's drawing into the syringe. I can't leave her."

Nancy went on working out who could be left the next day, and who could not. Fran only half listened. She was beginning to feel the warm air from the heater round her feet.

She was used to riding in the car with her mother. As a small child if she was ever unwell and away from school, Nancy would wrap her up warmly and take her on her rounds. She sat strapped into the front seat, surrounded by the mounds of equipment that Nancy carried with her: piles of absorbent sheets, packs of sterilised disposable instruments, tubs of green soap, rolls of bandages wrapped in dark blue, black medical bags. There was hardly room for her amongst it all.

On the windscreen was the blue and white District Nurse sign, which Fran used to think was a personal portrait of her mother. The front ledge below the wind-screen was always fascinating, a treasure trove of small tablet bottles, scissors, tweezers, syringes, thermometers, a stethoscope.

"What's this for, mum?" she would ask. "What do you do with this?"

And Nancy would always tell her.

But it was the smell of the car which was most evocative, the smell of soap and disinfectant and medicine, the smell of hospitals and surgeries. It was half attractive, half repellent; she always noticed it as soon as she got into the car, and it always took her back to when she was young.

It was the same smell, whichever car her mother was driving, but it reminded her most of the rounded, green Morris Minors. They were the only proper district nurses' cars; they all had white minis now.

Nancy was telling a story about one of the patients she had picked up that day. Fran watched the road ahead. They were out of the village and the headlights swept along snowy hedges and white trees. Suddenly her mother swung the wheel, the back of the car skidded round and they left the road and dived down a steep and narrow track.

"God, I nearly missed it!" she said.

Fran thought for a moment that the car was out of control, and grabbed the door, pressing her feet into the floor.

The car jolted up and down on the rocky surface of the lane, the exhaust clanking loudly. Sometimes they went over a stone that had rolled out of the bank, or into a pot-hole. Nancy slowed down. The brake lights shone red on the snow and reflected back into the interior of the car.

"I know I've been here before," said Nancy. "But I can't remember what it was for."

Gorse bushes growing out from the hedge scraped along the sides of the car, scattering their load of snow. The lane was sheltered, and there was not much snow on the ground. But suddenly ahead of them, in the lights of the car, was a great white barrier, where the snow blew through a gateway into the lane. They plunged into the drift and came out on the other side like a snow-plough. It was over before they realised what had happened.

Another five-barred gate showed up in the headlights; it looked as though it was right across the track. Nancy turned the car slowly in front of the gate, and the lights shone down what looked like a tunnel between the trees and bushes which grew across the path; there was no room for a car to pass through.

"This is where we get out and walk," she said. "I hope there's room to turn. I don't want to have to back all the way up."

She stopped the car and switched off the engine. It suddenly seemed very quiet. The only sound was the wind blowing round the car and through the trees.

Fran picked up a heavy rubber torch and Nancy reached into the back seat for her bag and a pile of incontinence pads. She switched off the car lights, and they were in complete darkness.

They got out of the car. The wind was driving the snow against them. Nancy put her arm through Fran's, and they set off together. Although the path was over-hung by trees, the snow had penetrated everywhere. It covered the ground, their footsteps pressing it firm.

The gorse bushes were thick with snow. Every twig and branch of the bare trees supported a layer several times its own thickness. The fir trees were all white.

A gust of wind would scatter snow from the bushes, and send a wave rushing along the path in front of them. Frances swept the beam of the torch from side to side.

There were no signs of any buildings or lights ahead of them. The path was still going down, but less steeply now as it followed the side of the hill. It became more and more overgrown, and in places they had to lower their heads to pass beneath the branches of trees, or hold back brambles until they had gone by.

Suddenly the torchlight shone below the level of the path upon snowy roofs and chimney pots overhung with trees. The track dipped steeply, and the two of them slithered over the snow into a courtyard. There were roofs with black gaps in them where the slates had fallen in, stable doors left open. Then they were at a back door, with a window on one side showing a faint light behind a blind.

Nancy opened the latch and walked straight in, calling in a loud voice, "Hullo! Is anyone at home?" Fran followed, and immediately found herself caught up in some sort of curtain. When she had extricated herself, she saw that she was in an old-fashioned farm kitchen with a beamed ceiling.

On the floor in front of the stove was a great heap of bedding, pillows, blankets and quilts. And sticking out of the pile was the tiny, wizened head of a very old woman. It was quite a brown head, with thin wisps of white hair. Her mouth was sunken and toothless.

An old man was standing, leaning with one hand on the kitchen table, where there were the remains of a meal.

"I'm some glad to see you," he said, with great deliberateness and sincerity.

Nancy stood still, just inside the door, and waited for him to recognise her.

"I'm glad you've come," he repeated, relieved that his waiting was over, but still not really noticing who was in the room.

"'Tis you!" said Nancy in her Cornish accent.

The old man looked puzzled. He was quite tall, with a face as brown as his wife's. His hair was just as white, though he had even less, a few long strands drawn across the top of his head. He had a long straight nose and a firm jaw which kept working up and down even when he was not talking.

"We've met before," said Nancy.

He tried hard to place her, a little anxious that he was being rude in not remembering her. "You haven't been here," he said.

"I have," said Nancy, not giving him much help.

"I've never had a day's illness in my life. Mrs Treloar had the nurse once, but 'twasn't you. 'Twas a much bigger woman, and older."

"What do you think of that then, Mrs Treloar?" said Nancy, going across to the old lady and kneeling beside her. "He doesn't remember me. I remember him all right!"

"Oh, well . . ." said the old lady gently.

"And what have you been doing, dear?"

"I fell . . . I was clearing the table, and the next thing I knew I was on the floor. I don't remember anything about it."

"She just went over, flat on her face," said Mr Treloar.

"Oh dear," said the old lady. "This is no way to receive visitors."

"We aren't visitors," said Nancy. "This is my daughter, she came to keep me company."

Fran shook hands with the old lady on the floor.

"I'm sorry . . . it's so humiliating . . . I don't know what I'll do."

"Now come on, dear. Let's get you to bed and make you nice and comfortable, and you'll soon feel better. You're lucky no bones have been broken."

"I don't know how we'll manage."

"Don't talk silly, Lettie!" said Mr Treloar with great firmness. "I can look after you."

Fran felt very out of place, now that she was here; she felt as though she was intruding upon the old people's misfortune. Unlike her mother, she had no part to play, and she stood awkwardly in front of the window and wished she was somewhere else.

She looked round the room. The ceiling—which was the wooden floor of the room above—had been painted a deep cream, and with the years it had turned smoky brown. There were metal hooks in the beams, where oil-lamps had once hung, though the kitchen was now lit by a single, low-watt electric light bulb, hanging from a flex in the central beam, with a simple plastic shade around it.

The stove was set in a large recess, the original open hearth of the farm. There was room for a chair on either side, and above the chimney was a long wooden mantel-piece, with a brown and white china dog at each end.

There were wooden chairs around a table, a window seat let into the thickness of the outside wall, a pine dresser with blue and white dinner plates on the shelves. The floor was of slate, with strips of carpet on it and there was a rag rug in front of the stove, alongside the old lady.

It smelt very unpleasant, but apart from that it was the sort of room that Fran liked. She could feel that it had been the centre of farm life for hundreds of years.

Her mother was busy with Mrs Treloar. She had sent the old man to fetch her night clothes. They could hear him going up the wooden stairs, very slowly, resting on each tread.

"Is there anything I could do?" asked Fran. She did not want to watch as her mother cleaned up the old lady.

"Have you got a hot-water bottle?" Nancy shouted.

"I'm not deaf, you know," the old lady said with great dignity.

"I'm sorry," said Nancy. "I get used to shouting at people. It's a bad habit . . . Have you got a bottle?"

"There should be one here," she said, feeling under the bedding.

Nancy pulled out an old stoneware bottle, the sort that Fran had seen only in antique shops. "Could you fill it up with hot water, and put it in her bed?"

Fran looked around.

"There's a kettle in the scullery."

She went back through the curtain and along a passage by the back door. She found a light-switch, and stood in the dim, freezing scullery, the old dairy of the farm. There was an electric kettle, and a sink with a cold tap.

By the time she had filled the bottle with hot water and taken it back to the kitchen, the old man had still not come down with the night clothes.

"See if you can bring them down quickly, Fran," said Nancy. "He may have forgotten what he went up for."

The old lady drew herself up, as far as she could on the floor. "Tom has a perfect memory," she said very deliberately.

Fran went up the stairs and stood on the landing. None of the light bulbs in the farm seemed stronger than forty watt. There was a door open down the passage-way. She went into the bedroom where the old man was standing holding on to the very solid wooden rail at the end of the bed. He had the clothes over his other arm.

"Shall I take them?" asked Fran, slipping the bottle into the bed.

"That'll be quicker," he said.

She took the night clothes down, and then went back to the scullery to make a pot of tea. She felt much happier now that she had something to do.

Then with Nancy on one side and Fran on the other, they got Mrs Treloar up the stairs, with a lot of pushing and laughing and nearly collapsing. Soon the old lady was lying comfortably in the big old mahogany bed, propped up on pillows, in the bare, freezing room.

Nancy sat on the edge of the bed and held her hands. "Squeeze my hand!" she said. "That's right. Now the other one."

Fran brought up the tea, and they all sat on the bed or on chairs. Their breath steamed in the cold room, and they drew warmth from the hot drink, holding both hands round the cups. There were no curtains at the windows, and the black night pressed against the panes. The wind sighed in the trees outside, and moaned in the chimney.

"Have you remembered me yet?" asked Nancy, looking across at the old man on the other side of the bed.

Immediately his face clouded. He had been looking relieved that his wife was safely in bed, but now the lines came back to his forehead.

"No, I can't say that I do," he said.

"I'll have to tell you then. Listen to this, Mrs Treloar, because he may never have told you about it. I was driving along the top road one day, in my nurse's car, and he flagged me down."

Mr Treloar suddenly slapped his leg loudly, and shouted out with immense vigour, "Dang it, 'tis you!"

" 'Tis me, you old rogue!" said Nancy. "And do you know what he wanted? He said, 'Nurse, what would you do with someone who has blood coming out of their stomach?' 'How's it coming out?' I asked. 'Is it a wound, or is it from down below?' 'It's like seeping out,' he said. 'Is it a man or a woman?' I asked. ' 'Tis a female,' he said. 'Would you have a look at her?' 'I suppose I'd better,' I said. So I left the car at the top and walked all the way down the lane, and when we got to the farm instead of coming through the door he took me to one of the sheds in the yard. 'There she is,' he said. It was a great fat sow!"

The old man threw back his head and roared with laughter, and the old lady joined in.

"I knew Cornish farmers didn't like spending money on vets, but I'd never known one to call in the district nurse before! The pig had a wound in its belly. I was so taken aback I cleaned it up, put on some antiseptic and taped it together. And he didn't remember me after all that!"

"It must be ten years ago," said Mr Treloar.

"He had his eyes on the pig, not on the district nurse. That's all he was bothered about!"

"You made a proper job of that wound, though. It healed up beautiful. I took her to market soon after."

"I bet you made a good price!"

"Not bad," he said, chuckling to himself.

Although it was so cold in the bedroom, the atmosphere was friendly and cheerful. Everyone seemed to be enjoying themselves.

But very soon Nancy made the excuse that Mrs Treloar needed to sleep, and they returned to the warmth of the kitchen. The old man took a long time to come down the stairs, but he refused any help, holding on to the banisters, chairbacks and the table-top until he could ease himself into the high, wooden arm-chair in the corner of the fireplace.

His eyes shone in the dark recess. He stared out like an animal in a cave, watchful and alert. He must have been a powerful man in his time; he still gave an impression of strength, even though he was so old. There was something primitive about him. He reminded Frances of ancient stones, an outcrop on top of a hill.

His hands were in the light, resting one across the back of the other in his lap. They were gnarled, the veins stood out in ridges. The tips of the fingers were thick and twisted, the skin shiny.

"I'll come and see you tomorrow," said Nancy. "Don't get up, we'll let ourselves out."

Fran looked back as she reached the curtain. His eyes glinted in the stone cavern. He raised one hand from his lap and held it, fingers splayed, in a gesture of benediction and farewell.

They plodded back up the lane, with the wind blowing into their faces. They pushed through the tangle of snow-covered bracken and brambles across the path, and reached the car. There was just room to back into the gateway and turn to face up the lane, but the wheels slipped on the snow and ice. Fran got out and pushed, the car set off up the lane, and she ran after it. Nancy stopped when she reached the road, and Fran jumped in.

She was thinking about the old couple, alone in the isolated farmhouse, one of them ill, the other hardly able to move.

"Why did she fall down?" she asked.

"She had a black-out."

"Why?"

"She had a slight stroke, I should think."

"Shouldn't she be in hospital?"

"Of course not! She's much better at home, she'd hate being in hospital."

"But he can't look after her very well."

"I'm more worried about him than I am about her," said Nancy. "He made out he was much fitter than he really was. Did you see his ankles?"

Fran had only noticed his hands.

"They were swollen, bulging over the edges of his shoes. He's got water in his legs."

"What does that mean?"

"It's a sign of heart failure. You're almost bound to get it in very old people. It will improve with rest, and he can have tablets for it. I'll put them both down for a visit from the doctor."

"But what will happen to them?"

"We can give them some support, and they'll muddle on. They'll be all right."

Fran felt that her mother was treating her like a child, hiding her real feelings and pretending to be cheerful and optimistic. She did not see how they could possibly be all right. As far as she could see, things could only get worse for them. The old man had hardly been able to climb the stairs. How could he look after his wife? They would have to struggle more and more to achieve less and less. It seemed terrible to have to face such problems when you were least able to deal with them.

Frances was having breakfast the next morning, eating her porridge in the kitchen and looking at the white world outside the window, when the phone rang. Her mother answered.

"Rosemary!" she said brightly. "You're early this morning!" Then her tone changed dramatically. "Oh I'm sorry . . . I see. Well, it's a release really, Jacky. You wouldn't have wanted her to go on suffering like that, would you? . . . Yes . . . I expect you'll have lots of relatives there . . . Well, if you really want me to, I'll look in this morning . . . Yes . . . Goodbye." She put down the receiver.

"Well, that's Amy Richards gone," she said.

The phone rang again almost immediately. This time it was the expected call.

Rosemary was young and had only just finished her training, and there was a certain amount of tension between the two nurses. Nancy believed in doing everything for the convenience of the patients, Rosemary tried to impose hospital standards upon them. If an old man wanted his dog on the bed, Nancy would say, Why not? Rosemary would give him a lecture on hygiene and chase it outside. Fran felt rather sorry for Rosemary, she did not stand much chance.

Nancy opened her large diary, and they went through the work for the day.

"Mrs Richards has gone," she said. Fran watched her put a stroke in her book, like a recording angel.

"Mr Hosking's gone . . . Mr Borlase has gone." She struck through the names in her black and gold-lettered diary.

"You're doing well, Mum," said Fran.

Nancy glanced up, not certain whether there had been an interruption or not. She went on with the distribution of the work.

"Mrs Keast has come out of hospital with bed sores . . . Yes, it's always the same. When I was in hospital we would have been ashamed to send a patient home the way they come out now . . . If I do Keast, would you do Tremayne? Then you might as well do Clemo. You know, the little lady who lost her husband?"

How very careless of her, thought Fran.

"I'll do Jenkin. What do you make of Mrs Pengilly? I think she's very much better, she was toddling around like a two-year-old yesterday, dusting her room. It's time we pulled out of there."

Fran was used to hearing Nancy on the phone in the background. A lot of it flowed over her, a jumble of names of patients and drugs, and every now and again she would suddenly find herself listening to some arresting item or catching one of her mother's expressions. 'It's time we pulled out' was one that often cropped up. It created a vivid picture in Fran's mind of a military operation, with a convoy of trucks evacuating an outpost, Nancy at the wheel.

The pencil moved down the list. "Mr Spargo . . . He could hardly breathe yesterday. He asked me how long he'd live. 'Why on earth do you think I can give you an answer to that!' I said. 'You've got to take it from day to day. Make the most of it, enjoy what you can. You've had your bowels open this morning—that's enough joy for one day!' The poor fellow laughed at that—he's obsessed with his bowels, isn't he? . . . Well yes, they all are. But for a man of his age, not yet fifty . . .

"By the way, there was a message from Frank Pascoe in the surgery. Would the nurse deliver his tablets? I told him when I saw him, we're trained nurses, not errand boys. I don't mind taking prescriptions for someone who can't get out, but he's always driving round the village. He can fetch his own tablets."

Rosemary was making noises suggesting total agreement at the other end of the line. Fran suspected that she had been taking Frank Pascoe his tablets, and that Nancy was telling her to stop it.

"I picked up another couple last night, after I got back from Amy Richards." Nancy picked up even more often than she pulled out. "A Mr and Mrs Treloar, they've been muddling on long after they're capable of looking after themselves. We'll have to sort something out for them today . . . Right, I'll see you at the surgery, about eleven o'clock. Bye."

Fran put on her coat, scarf and gloves, pushed her feet into her boots, and carrying her bag with her school books and indoor shoes, walked up the road to the bus-stop. There was a covering of snow everywhere, but several cars had been through and there were clear tracks along the road. Nevertheless, there was an air of excitement in the street. The children waiting for the school bus were all over the road. Some were sliding, others smashing ice on the puddles. A lot were throwing snowballs, and it was not long before Fran felt a thud against her back. She turned round, but the boys were too far away for her to reach them. She walked on with her shoulders raised, expecting a snowball in the back of the neck at any moment. But none came.

Everyone was talking about whether the bus would arrive. As soon as it was a minute or two overdue, a lot of the children disappeared to their homes, or to the homes of their friends if they thought that their parents might drive them to school. Some children said it was official; one of the mothers had rung the bus company and they said none of their buses was leaving the depot.

So after a few minutes, Fran walked home as well.

Nancy was just leaving.

"They stop running for any excuse," she said. "It's not too bad, it won't stop me."

She leaned out of the car window, to reverse into the road. She had the choke out and the engine was roaring; there were clouds of smoke coming from the exhaust.

"I'll be back for lunch," she called.

The car moved off towards the village, enveloped in fumes which rose into the snowy sky.

Fran went up to her bedroom and changed out of her school clothes into jeans and a heavy jumper. She wondered whether to tidy her room. Although Nancy sometimes seemed rather disorganised, her room at the front of the house was very neat, while Fran, who seemed normally neat and tidy, left her bedroom at the back of the house in a complete muddle. She decided against sorting it out.

She made some coffee. The telephone rang.

"I'm sorry, she's just left for work . . . She'll be at the surgery at eleven."

It sounded like the matron again.

She picked up her book and sat close to the stove, looking out through the window at the grey sky and the white roof of the house opposite. It had a closed-up look; all the curtains were drawn to keep out the cold. She drank her coffee slowly, and enjoyed the feeling of being able to take her time, the break from routine. She did not start reading.

She kept thinking about Mr Treloar. She could see his bright blue eyes staring out from the dark fireplace. She wondered how he was managing in the lonely farmhouse. She wondered what it looked like in daylight. She thought that in the afternoon she might walk there. She would not go inside, but she would like to see where they had gone in the dark last night.

She read all morning and at one o'clock heated a tin of tomato soup and cut the bread ready for toast. She did not really expect her mother back, because Nancy was always optimistic about finishing at a certain time, and nearly always something cropped up to delay her. But a few minutes after one o'clock she heard the car roar up to the garage and the engine stop. Almost immediately there was a heavy bump on the door, and Nancy rushed in.

She went straight to the phone. "I must make a quick call," she explained. "I should just catch him." She dialled, and waited.

"Hullo, is that my favourite undertaker? . . . I've got another job for you . . . What do you mean, you're exhausted! I'm not keeping you busy, blame the weather . . . Anyway, do you know dear little Mrs Richards? . . . Yes, that's right . . . There's just one thing, Jacky her husband is being a bit peculiar. He doesn't want to let her go out of the house. He won't hear of a chapel of rest, he wants to leave her there on the bed. Well, normally it would be all right in this weather, but he's lit a blazing fire in the room. He's taking everyone in to see her . . . Yes, I think she ought to be screwed down as soon as possible. Just see what you can do . . . Thanks!"

"Your soup's ready," said Fran.

"Sorry, I must just spend a quick penny," said Nancy, and she rushed up the stairs to the bathroom.

When she came down she sighed with relief. "That's better!" she said. "Everywhere I went this morning, they offered me a cup of tea, because of the weather. I don't like to refuse." She sat down to her soup and toast. "How have you got on?"

"I've read all morning."

"Any calls?"

"Just one from the matron."

30

"That bloody matron, I'll wring her neck! She's been chasing me all morning, she rang the surgery twice. She's got this woman who's dying, and two weeks ago the doctor said she wouldn't last a few days. Now of course she's blaming her for not being dead. I do wish doctors wouldn't say that someone only has so long to go. They only do it because they see doctors on television saying things like 'I'm afraid your husband has only three months to live.' It makes them feel like little gods. No one ever knows. This lady's very frail, but she could go on for weeks."

"Have you seen the old couple at the farm?"

"I haven't had time yet," said Nancy. "I've only just come from the surgery. When we were there, Frank Pascoe came in for his tablets, the ones I wouldn't deliver to him yesterday. He looked really angry. He came up to the receptionist's window and banged on the glass. 'Where are my tablets?' he shouted. She asked him to sit down but he went on shouting, so she asked Doctor Turner to see him. He went in shouting 'Where are my tablets?' and you could hear Turner shouting back 'Don't shout at me! I'm not your bloody grocer!' But he got his tablets, without waiting for them."

"Are you going to Penhallow?"

"Yes."

"Can I come with you?"

"If you want to," said Nancy, rather surprised. "I should be glad of your company. I might need someone to push me up the hill again."

The streets were slushy when they set out. The wheels of the car swished along the road they had taken the previous evening, but now Fran could see the snowy mound of the hill above Stennack and beyond it a narrow band of dark grey sea.

They drove out of the village and along the coast, past

the ruins of engine houses in a derelict mining area. The snow which had stuck on the sides of the chimneys looked like the remains of white lettering. They could no longer see the sea, although they were following the line of the cliffs.

It was a mile or two to the farm, and this time Nancy slowed down well before the turning. The car crawled down the track. Fran could see nothing but the high banks on either side, topped with gorse and thorn bushes. But as they approached the gate where they had parked on the previous evening, there was a sense of space beyond. As soon as the car stopped, she jumped out and ran to the gate, wondering what she would see at the other side.

The gateway overlooked a deep valley, with low trees, willows and alders, around a stream. The other side was covered with dead bracken and heather which the snow had not completely obliterated. The end of the valley was a deep V, filled with the slate-grey sea. There were several mining buildings near the coast, engine houses and chimneys, covered with snow.

"Come on, Fran!" called Nancy. "I could do with some help."

"Come and look, Mum!" said Fran.

So Nancy joined her at the gate and looked into the valley.

It seemed strange to Fran that although it was so near her home she had never seen it before. She had been to the beach at the end, approaching it from the coastal path. But there was no road through the valley, and it remained cut off and unknown.

They could not see the farmhouse. It was further inland, tucked into the hillside and surrounded by trees, sheltered from all directions.

"Isn't it beautiful!"

"It's a bit out of the way," said Nancy.

"I'd love to live here!"

"I wouldn't like getting the car out every morning."

The wind was blowing down the valley from the north, and a gust swirled through the gateway. Nancy shivered. "Come on!" she said.

They plunged into the tunnel between the bushes. Their footprints were still in the snow from the previous evening. No one else had been down the track to the farm.

Where the path turned steeply down the hillside, the buildings came into view. The house was built of stone, great blocks of brown and grey slatestone, with pieces of granite at the corners, and granite lintels over the door and windows. The farm-buildings were also stone-built, and looked as solid as the house, though there was an air of neglect about them.

At the door, Fran hesitated. She had only really wanted to see the place in daylight. She did not want to go inside again; she would rather see if there was a footpath to the beach.

But her mother had hurried into the house, and Fran was carrying one of her bags, so she had to take it in. She entered the kitchen. It was very dim inside, the light from the window hardly reaching the far corners. Sitting next to the stove, in the same wooden chair as last night, was Mr Treloar.

Nancy had gone straight upstairs. Fran put the bag on the table. She felt that she could not simply walk out, and yet she would feel awkward if she stayed. It was difficult talking to old people. Nancy could do it, she was used to it. But Fran had nothing to say.

"Good afternoon," she said.

The old man put his head to one side, and leaned forward. He had not heard.

"Good afternoon," shouted Fran, her heart sinking.

He nodded his head.

33

"Snow," she shouted, jabbing her finger at the window.

No, she thought, it's better not to say anything. She could not do an imitation of Nancy.

His jaws were working up and down, as though he was chewing, though he said nothing. He began to pull himself out of his chair.

"No, don't disturb yourself!" said Fran, quite alarmed at the effort he was making. He might fall down.

He straightened himself, and slowly reached up on to the mantelpiece. He felt what he was looking for, and brought down a small wooden box. He held it out to Fran.

"Look!" he said.

She waited for him to settle back into his chair. She looked at the box; it was made of dark oak, with a lid. A box for cigarettes or trinkets.

Again she was reminded of the days when she was much younger and used to go out with her mother. Old people would find some object to amuse her, a pocket watch or a medal.

"Open it!" he said, with a smile.

She took off the lid, and almost screamed. Inside the box were the severed heads of two birds, feathery and long-billed.

"Ugh!" she went.

"Pick them up!" said Mr Treloar.

Gingerly, she picked one out. It weighed almost nothing at all, just a dried-out ball of tawny feathers, glazed eyes, and a long bill.

"Is it a curlew?"

"They're woodcock."

"What do you keep them for?" she asked, but he did not hear her.

"I've seen flocks of them come in over the sea," he said, "and they've been so exhausted they couldn't rise over the cliffs. They had to rest on the beach. Sometimes the rocks were covered with them."

She put back the bird's head and gave him the box.

"Put it on the table," he said. "We'll show it to Nurse." There was a light in his eyes. He seemed to enjoy surprising people with his decapitated woodcock.

"When I was a boy, I remember going to school one day and I met the parson. He had his gun with him, and he was looking for some sport. 'Have you seen any birds, boy?' he says to me. 'Yes, sir,' I says, 'I've seen snipe and woodcock and whistlers.' 'Show me where they are, and I'll make it right with your teacher.'"

"What's a whistler?" asked Fran.

"A whistler?" said Mr Treloar. When he asked a question he sounded very fierce. He thought about it for a while and Fran thought that she was not going to get an answer. Then he said, "A whistler is a golden plover. There used to be enormous flocks of plover in the old days, many more than now. There's still plenty of pee-wits, but you hardly ever see a whistler."

Fran noticed that there was a bird-table hanging outside the window, and robins and blue-tits were coming and going. One fluttered against the glass for a moment.

When Nancy came downstairs, she stood in front of Mr Treloar, her hands on her hips, and shook her head. "Did you go to bed last night, Mr Treloar?" she asked accusingly.

He pointed to the box on the table. "Look at that!" he said.

She picked up the box casually. "His side of the bed hasn't been touched," she said to Fran. "I bet he slept in that chair." She opened the box, and shrieked.

"They're horrid!" she said, drawing her arms in tight to her sides, and generally reacting as women are supposed to react to spiders and mice, to small furry or feathery creatures, but acting it up quite a bit. Mr Treloar found her performance very satisfying. His chest heaved up and down as he laughed to himself.

"Mr Treloar, when did you last sleep in your bed?" she persisted.

He did not understand her.

"How long have you been sleeping in that chair?"

"Yes," said Mr Treloar. "I sleep very well."

"Mr Treloar, you're not as deaf as you make out," said Nancy. "You can hear when you want to." She moved to his other side. "I reckon you've got a good side," she said. "You can hear with this ear, can't you?"

"That's my good ear," he admitted.

Nancy pulled up a chair and sat down close to him, speaking into his left ear. She placed a hand on his arm. "Can you hear me all right?" she asked, without shouting.

"Yes, I can hear you."

"It's very important for you to go to bed," she said, pronouncing her words very clearly. "You've got to get your legs up. The swelling will go down if you give them a rest."

The old man pressed his lips together, so that his mouth made one stubborn line.

"Do you find it difficult getting upstairs?"

"I like my chair by the fire."

"Let me have a look round," said Nancy. "Do you mind if I see what rooms you've got? I won't be long."

She went out to the hall, and the old man sat nodding his head, the corners of his mouth pulled down. He gazed into the distance.

"Talking of woodcock," he said suddenly, in a way which startled Fran, "there used to be a dam across the top of the valley, to conserve a supply of water for the tin works. This silted up, and some fishermen planted willows, which they used for making lobster-pots and crab-pots. That was a wonderful place for woodcock."

Nancy came back from her quick tour of inspection. She put her face close to the side of his head and held his hand.

"You've got a lovely sitting-room across the hall," she said. "I think it would be a good idea to have your bed put in there."

Mr Treloar certainly heard, for he turned his head sharply and looked at Nancy. He did not seem to like the idea.

"It would be much easier while Mrs Treloar is in bed. You wouldn't have to go upstairs to her, and the toilet's on the ground floor. You could sleep in bed at night, and get those feet up!"

He pressed his lips firmly together again as he thought about this.

"And I see you've got an electric point in there. You could have an electric fire. Mrs Treloar needs some warmth, you know."

Mr Treloar shook his head.

"Well, you think about it," said Nancy. "Talk about it to the doctor when he comes, see what he thinks about it . . . Do you have any relatives?"

"We've got a grandson."

"Does he ever come and see you?"

"About once a month."

"He could move your bed down for you, couldn't he?"

She turned to Fran. "We'll have to get hold of him. It's the relatives who ought to do things like this." Then she turned back to Mr Treloar. "You could do with some help in the house. Shall I get a home help for you?"

Again he turned sharply to look into her face.

"I can find a nice lady who will come in for an hour or two, a few times a week."

"I don't want anyone in the house," said the old man.

"Are you worried about the expense?" asked Nancy.

Mr Treloar crashed his fist down on the arm of his

chair. "I'm not short of a pound or two," he said. "I'll pay for what we need."

"Mr Treloar," said Nancy. "How do you manage for shopping?"

"Mr Laity, up at the top farm, fetches our pension for us. He's been doing the shopping too."

"And how old is he?"

"Oh, he's a young man," said Mr Treloar. Then he looked up and his eyes twinkled. "He's in his sixties," he added.

"How do you keep the stove alight?" asked Nancy.

"I fetch the coal."

"Where from?"

"The coalman only comes halfway down the lane," Mr Treloar admitted. "So I fetch the coal from there."

"You mean you go up that lane, in this weather, carrying buckets of coal!" exclaimed Nancy. "A home help would do all that for you. She'd fetch the coal and keep the stove going, she'd get your shopping and cook you a meal. It would make all the difference."

He looked very doubtful.

"Shall I fill up the coal-buckets?" asked Fran.

Mr Treloar looked from Nancy to her, knowing that she had interrupted but not knowing what she had said. When he saw her picking up the coal-hod, he started to make objections, but Nancy told her to go ahead.

Fran carried two empty hods up the lane as far as the parked car. Right opposite was a wooden coal-bunker, hidden from sight by a covering of snow. The sides were thick with ivy; each leaf held a scoop of snow, with the green outline of the leaf visible around the edge.

She dug into the hole at the base of the bunker, and the coal came tumbling out on to the white ground. She tried to separate coal and snow.

As she went back down the lane, balancing the buckets on each side, she thought of old Mr Treloar fetching the coal each day. Getting dressed to go out, climbing up the steep path, carrying the heavy buckets when his legs were painful to walk on—all of these demanded an enormous effort. Even the most ordinary things that everyone else took for granted, like getting undressed and going to bed, became as much as a day's work when you were old.

She placed the hods near the stove and he thanked her with a courtesy which seemed old-fashioned, an insistence on making quite clear to her how grateful he was.

"It was nothing," she murmured. She knew he never heard anything she said.

Nancy had been talking to him about her other patients of his age, to see which ones he knew.

"How is it you know all the old rogues?" she asked.

His eyes twinkled. "I reckon you've got to be a bit of a rogue to live to ninety!"

Nancy laughed. "Do you know Frank Pascoe?"

"Frank Pascoe?" he repeated fiercely. "I know *him*." He clamped his lips firmly together.

"Don't you like him?"

"Huh!" he uttered, grinding his jaws. "He's only interested in money."

"He's got a home help!"

"I bet you," said Mr Treloar with great force, "he don't pay for her!"

"He doesn't, he gets all he can out of the Social Services. He says he hasn't got a penny."

"That's a lie! He owned Stennack Town Farm at one time. If I have a home help, I shall pay for her myself."

"So you've decided to have a home help," said Nancy.

"I'll think about it," he said.

Nancy went back to say goodbye to Mrs Treloar, and Fran started to go. At the curtain she turned round. The old man was sitting in the recess. He gave her a wink.

★

39

"I know just the woman for them," said Nancy when they were back in the car. "Mavis Bray's a bit rough and ready, but she's got a good heart. You couldn't send her to some places, but I think she'd get on well with Mr Treloar. I'll have a word with the home help organiser when we get back."

Fran wondered how it felt, to know that you were moving downstairs and never going back up again. To be retreating into two rooms, when you had once had the freedom of the valley and the seashore. To give up fetching your own wood and coal, even though it had been a struggle. To have a helper coming into your home. To give up your independence.

"It seems a shame," she said.

"It comes to everyone sooner or later. And it's come to them later than most," said Nancy. "They've still got each other, they're in their own home. They've gone on as long as they can on their own. Now they've got to have some help."

"It's a shame to become dependent, though."

Nancy took it as a personal criticism. "What else could we do?" she asked. "We haven't put them into hospital, we haven't even upset their routine immediately, I've only suggested they move downstairs and have a home help. You tell me how we could treat them more humanely!"

"I don't know," admitted Fran.

"It's sad," said Nancy. "But that's old age."

"How long can they go on?" Fran asked.

"I don't know," said Nancy, still slightly irritated. "You're talking like all the relatives. As soon as they've got an elderly parent to look after, they put on a long face and they say, 'How long will it be, Nurse?' If I think they're wondering how long they've got to put up with the old man, I say very cheerfully, 'Oh, he'll go on like this for years!' And if I think they're after his money, I say, 'He'll probably outlive you, my dear!' You can't tell. Either of them could have a massive stroke tonight and be gone by tomorrow. But I don't think they will. They're pretty tough, these ninety-year-olds. They've got to be to have lasted so long."

Fran thought of the Forsaken Indian Woman. Too old and frail to keep up with the tribe, she became a burden to them. She was given enough fuel and enough food to last a few days, and then she was left by her fire in the snow as the tribe moved on and the wolves howled.

"I don't want to be old," she said.

Her mother dropped her at the house, and then went off in the car again. Fran took the local paper out of the letter box, and unlocked the door. She lit the fire in the sitting-room. Nancy had stuck nursing tape over the joins in the window frame, but the draught still cut through the room like a knife.

One of the hospitals rang with details of a patient who was being discharged, and would the nurse check the wound? The matron of the private home rang, and did her mother have a list of night-sitters? Nancy would explode! An old man rang and asked if the nurse was all right, as they had not seen her for some days. Fran wrote down his name and address.

She did not feel like reading or playing a tape. She sat by the fire and looked into the flames. She began to feel that she was becoming obsessed with morbid thoughts.

She had always heard about people dying, for as long as she could remember. When she was at the village school, she had been asked what her mother's job was, and she had replied that it was helping people to die.

But it was only recently that her mother had started talking so openly about her work to her. Once she had started, she had quickly got into the way of telling her everything. And though Fran liked to share her confi-

41

dences, she did not really want to hear all that she was told. Without realising what was happening, she dwelt more and more upon Nancy's accounts of her day-to-day activities. Expressions like *senile dementia . . . psychogeriatrics . . . terminal cancer* would come unbidden into her mind. It became more real to her than school.

When Nancy came in, she switched on the light. "What are you doing, sitting in the dark?" she asked.

"I was just thinking."

Nancy drew the curtains, which billowed outwards in the draught, and picked up the paper. "I'll get a meal in a minute," she said, sitting down in front of the fire. "I'll just have a look at the deaths."

"Oh no!" said Fran

"What's the matter?"

"It's so ghoulish!"

"It's not," said Nancy.

"But to look at the deaths before anything else, it's morbid!"

"I always read the deaths first," said Nancy. She found the obituaries and the deaths column, and turned the page back. "It's simply professional. There are no lists sent to the surgery, and I'm always meeting people in the street and I say cheerfully, 'Hullo, Mrs Penhaligon, how's your husband?' And she puts on a long face and says, 'Didn't you know, nurse? He's been dead three weeks.' I feel so embarrassed." The paper crackled. "Oh, Mr Penrose has died. He didn't last long then, once he went to hospital."

"Do you ever cure anyone, Mum?" Fran asked.

"Of course I do!" said Nancy. "I saw Mrs Gribble's toenail today. It looked marvellous, I felt really pleased with it. And I've got a way with ulcers. If they haven't been left too late I can usually clear them up. I have a lot of successes—people who come out of hospital after operations get better. I even cure their bed-sores."

42

"But you have a lot of hopeless cases."

"The successes go off my list, the hopeless ones stay, that's all."

"Until they die."

"It was better on the district in the old days," admitted Nancy. "Then you had as many births as deaths. But now the births take place in hospital on Mondays to Fridays, between nine and five. You only get a few individualists who stick out for home confinement. That used to make the work more varied. But I wouldn't want to work in a hospital. It's still real nursing on the district, it's you and your patient."

She turned to the *In Memoriam* column. "'In loving memory of my dear husband Alfie,'" she read out. "'Sadly missed'—and she couldn't stand him when he was alive!"

Fran looked at the other side of the paper that her mother was holding. In large print it announced the films that were showing that week in the local cinemas: DEATH ON THE NILE and THE GAME OF DEATH.

Later in the evening they sat by the sitting-room fire, watching a film on television. It was a historical drama, ending with the death of a king. His eyes suddenly stared, his head jerked back, and a dark liquid spilled from his mouth on their black and white screen.

"I bet it looks good in colour," said Fran. Then she added, "Does it really happen like that?"

"Of course not," said Nancy. "I've never seen anyone die the way they do on television. Dying is very hard work, it takes a long time. But nowadays most people are heavily sedated when they die, and they don't know anything about it. I think some of them could be much more conscious of what's happening, and would like to be. But we give the drugs for the sake of the relatives, not for the patient. It's the relatives who can't bear it."

43

"Mum," asked Fran. "How do you feel when one of your patients dies?"

"It depends," said Nancy. "I know you think I'm quite heartless about it. Amy Richards has gone, tick her off the book, that's one less to do today!"

"No, I don't think that."

"I'm glad Amy died, I wouldn't have wanted her to go on suffering. But I'm sad too, because I nursed her for a long time, and she was a brave woman . . . If it's someone you hardly know, it doesn't mean anything. But if it's someone you've nursed all through their illness, then you get close to them and you feel it deeply. I don't mind too much if I feel someone's had a good life and I've made them as comfortable as I can at the end. But I hate it when I feel people have been cheated, and then I get very angry. I feel angry about Mr Spargo. He's got asbestosis. When he was in the Navy he used to line boilers with asbestos. The Navy say they'll review his case in six months time. He'll be dead by then, and he's not yet fifty . . . I hate it when children die . . . And I think the mother of a young family is even worse. A young person puts up such a struggle to live. I remember Judith, I was with her all the time. She fought and fought against dying. And on the morning of the day she died she started her period. It seemed so relentless, nature giving and taking without any care. You feel so helpless . . .

"I don't think you ever get hardened to it, Fran. At least, I don't. But you have to seem to be, just to keep going. You've got other patients to look after, and they expect you to be in control of your feelings. You've got to give strength to them. But sometimes, when I'm in bed at night, I grieve for them. I shall probably weep for Amy Richards, though you wouldn't believe it."

The school bus was running again the next day, and a storm of rain washed most of the snow away. Nancy was

44

in the kitchen when Fran returned home. She was trying to catch up on her paperwork, and the table was spread with green, pink and white forms and scraps of paper with sums on them. Nancy had an air of desperation about her; she would much rather be out dealing with people, whatever sort of mess they were in, than with pieces of paper. There was a box of Black Magic chocolates open in front of her.

"Add up these figures for me, love," she sighed, after Fran had made a pot of tea and placed it amongst the confusion on the table. "I can't get them to tally."

She went on copying details from her black book on to the forms. "How have you got on today?"

"All right," said Fran.

She added up the columns of figures, and came to the same result as Nancy. "They're correct," she said.

"They don't agree with the mileometer," said her mother. She looked through the daily mileages in her book again. "Anything happen?"

Fran tried to think of something interesting to say about school. She went back over the day in her mind, the bus arriving outside the main entrance, the run through the rain, crowded corridors and metal lockers, the smell of wet clothing.

"No," she said.

Nancy laughed. "That took you a long time!"

"I was trying to think."

She knew Nancy would have something to tell her; every day produced a fund of stories. This often puzzled Fran. Life to her seemed a continuous series of impressions, none of which could be easily separated from the rest and recounted. But for Nancy everything seemed to happen in neat packages.

She had already started an anecdote.

"I went to see Mrs Tregidga's leg," she said. "She's gone right out of her mind. Quite cuckoo! She sat there

45

hooting with laughter as I took down her stockings. The night before last she got up at three in the morning and started to cook a meal. Her husband—he's eighty-seven —tried to stop her, they had a real ding-dong battle."

"What did you do?" asked Fran.

"I told her daughter to go down to the surgery and tell the doctor. I think Jacky's going a bit peculiar, too. I saw him briefly, he gave me the chocolates. Anyway, he's had Amy put in a chapel of rest, thank goodness. 'It's a good job I got her to sign her pension book up to Easter,' he said. 'Jacky!' I said. 'You can't go on drawing her pension!' 'Do you think they'd take it away from me?' 'They'd put you in prison!' I said."

She pushed the box of chocolates across the table to Fran. When someone died, the relatives often felt that they wanted to give a small present to the nurse. It was nearly always a box of Black Magic chocolates. The name seemed appropriate and the black wrapping had a suitably funereal aspect. Fran wondered if the makers realised that they had captured this small corner of the market.

"Then I went into the stores," Nancy went on. "I wanted to get a walking frame for Mr Treloar, it'll help him to get about more easily. Whilst I was there I had a good look round and I found just the thing for Mrs Vivian—a raising table. She could stand it by her wheel-chair and all she'd have to do is touch a lever and it would come to the right height for her. It would make all the difference. I was delighted. I was just going to take it— Mr Opie always lets me have whatever I want—when he said, 'Look out, here comes the boss!' and this man came in. I'd never seen him before. So I explained that I wanted it for a paraplegic woman, confined to a wheel-chair, thirty-years-old with two children—laying it on a bit. And he said, 'Is it an aid for living?' 'It's not an aid for dying,' I said. 'No,' he said, 'would it be a help to her?' 'Of course it would!' I said. 'Then I'm afraid you can't

46

have it,' he said. 'You can only have aids for nursing. Aids for living have to come from the Social Services.' Would you believe it? 'Well,' I said, 'it would be an aid for nursing too. I could put the bowl on it when I'm washing her.' So he let me have it."

As she told the story she kept on copying names from her book on to the forms.

"Did you see Mr and Mrs Treloar today?" Fran asked, biting into a chocolate.

Nancy laughed. "That was funny," she said. "I went by the kitchen window and then instead of going into the house, I went back to the window and looked in. I don't know why, to show him I was bringing his frame, I think. And there was Mr Treloar, his head down, struggling to get his foot up on to a stool with a cushion on it. So I took my time, and then went in. He looked a bit red in the face, but very pleased with himself. 'I've been doing what you said, nurse,' he said. 'I've got my foot up.' 'Let's have a look at it,' I said. So I pulled up his trouser leg and looked. I pretended to study it very seriously. 'I wouldn't say that leg had been up more than two minutes,' I said. 'How do 'ee know that, Nurse?' he said. 'I can tell by looking at it,' I said. He looked at me, he didn't know whether I was teasing him or not. 'There's no fooling you, is there?' he said. 'Only once,' I said. 'You won't fool me a second time!'

"His shoes were cutting into his ankles and hurting him a lot. So I said, 'Let me cut them down a bit for you!' I took them off him, and had a pair of scissors and cut them down each side. He put them on again and said, 'That's much better, a proper job!' And then he said, 'I thought you were going to mutilate them.' "

"Mutilate?"

"That's what he said, and he said it with a sort of relish. He's got a feeling for words, I've noticed it with other things he's said . . . Anyway, I told him if he didn't want his legs to look like skittles for the rest of his life, he'd better get them up . . . Mrs Treloar was very much better. She can get up and wash herself each day now, and come down for a few hours. And they agreed to have the bed downstairs, so before they could change their minds I rang the grandson, and his wife answered. They're coming over at the weekend to move the furniture . . . The old man sent you a message, by the way. He always refers to you as 'the maid', and he seems to think you are interested in bird-life. He said 'Tell the maid that a pair of peregrine falcons used to nest on the cliffs at the end of the valley, year after year.' "

"There aren't any left now."

"He wanted to talk about them, but I couldn't stop. He's full of stories of birds and animals and the sea. I wish I could give him more time."

It was Nancy's weekend on duty—she had every other weekend off—and on Saturday afternoon she decided to look in at the farm, to see how the move was going.

"Would you like to come with me?" she asked.

Fran said that she would. She still wanted to walk down the valley to the sea.

"It was Amy Richards's funeral this morning," Nancy said as they drove past the village cemetery. "The whole procession was lined up outside the gates. As I went by, they were just getting back into their cars. Jacky was there, in a brown overcoat with a black arm-band, and all the relatives. My instinct when I see anyone I know is to give a cheery wave, and I couldn't stop myself. They all looked back very solemnly."

They passed the farm on the coast road, and then turned down into the lane. Fran saw a red car parked by the gate at the bottom. It surprised her to see it there, though she realised that the relatives were bound to come by car. In her mind the place was always cut off from

48

the outside world. She resented the car a little bit.

Nancy parked in the lane, above the red car, and they walked down the path. All the snow had gone, except for a few patches under the banks.

Water was running beneath the stones of the path, and in some places it was muddy. Their attention was given to avoiding the mud and holding aside the branches, and they were right above the house before they heard the shouting. They both stopped and looked down into the yard. From inside the house came a voice raised in anger. It went on and on.

Nancy looked at Fran. "What's going on?" she asked.

She hurried down the steep slope into the yard and up to the back door. Fran followed. The shouts of anger continued, punctuated by loud bangs.

Inside the kitchen Mr Treloar was standing in front of his chair. He held his walking stick by the end, and was bringing down the flat of the handle on the kitchen table.

"I won't have it!" he shouted, swinging his arm down and beating the table-top. His eyes were blazing, and the veins stood out on his forehead. By the door to the hall stood a heavy, rather florid, middle-aged man and a stout woman. They turned round.

"I tell 'ee—" shouted Mr Treloar, and then he stopped short, his arm raised. He saw Nancy and Fran standing just inside the curtain. In the silence which followed, the voice of Mrs Treloar could be heard calling from upstairs.

Nancy stood and looked at him across the table. "What's all this, Mr Treloar?" she asked quietly.

He dropped back into his chair and his walking stick clattered to the floor. He pressed his lips together and worked his jaws. He looked as black as thunder.

The other two people shifted awkwardly. They must be the grandson and his wife, thought Fran. She had only thought of grandchildren as young people, and was surprised that Desmond and Vera Rowe were quite old. The atmosphere in the room was thick with tension, and she wanted to get out, but dared not move.

Nancy went across to the old man and took his hand. "You'll make yourself ill," she said. "You must calm down."

The granddaughter-in-law spoke up. "I think they ought to be in a home," she said. "I think it's disgusting leaving them to look after themselves here."

"Good!" said Nancy brightly. "Are you offering to take them?"

"We couldn't have them!" Mrs Rowe said indignantly. "We haven't got the room. They ought to be in Goonlaze House."

She spoke loudly, and Mr Treloar caught the name of the old people's home. "I'm not going to Goonlaze House!" he said, sounding as though he was going to begin shouting again. "I'm not going in to the Union!"

"Now then, Mr Treloar, don't start that again!" said Nancy. "Because no one is sending you to Goonlaze House. You can't go there if you don't want to."

"They can't manage here!" said Vera Rowe. "It's quite ridiculous!"

"They can decide for themselves. The law says that no one can be put into hospital against their will. If they aren't capable of deciding, a doctor can apply to the magistrates to have them committed, and I've only known that happen once or twice. Mr Treloar is quite able to make up his own mind."

"I won't have it!" said Mr Treloar. "I won't have them coming in here and telling me what to do! I'm not going to end my days in the Workhouse!"

"We're only thinking what's best for you, Grandad," said Mrs Rowe.

"I'll decide what's best for me! I won't have you telling me what to do."

"Mr Treloar, I'm surprised at you," said Nancy.

"They've given up their afternoon to help you. That's no way to speak to them."

"I've paid them," said the old man. "I've paid for their petrol and their time. I pay them every time they come here. I want that furniture shifted. And Desmond, I want the path cleared. I don't want Nurse having to push her way through the brambles."

"Yes, Grandad," said Mr Rowe. It was the first time he had spoken.

"Let's get the furniture sorted out to begin with," said Nancy. "And I expect you'd like a walk down the valley, wouldn't you, Fran?"

"Oh yes," said Fran, relieved to escape.

The farm was built on a ledge in the hillside. She walked round the side of the house and found herself in a tangled garden. The long grass had been flattened by the snow; bushes and shrubs had grown wild, and branches straggled over the lawn and path. There were walled terraces on one side, with broken statuary.

The garden looked over the valley, but the trees below had grown up to obscure the view. A path wound through them, and she followed it down to the stream, which was crossed by a wooden bridge with a hand-rail. She walked on through a wood of low trees, thick with lichen and covered with ivy. The small oaks still retained their dead, brown leaves.

The path came out of the wood and crossed the stream again. It was more exposed to the sea winds here. The gorse bushes had grown top-heavy, and with the weight of the snow many of them had collapsed, their stems snapped and the bushes lying across the path. The dead gorse was pale, almost colourless.

As she dropped lower into the valley it widened and its character changed. The fields of the farm came to an end, and on both sides mine waste spread into the bracken, blue stone rubble brought up from underground. There were the remains of buildings, with a few ivy-covered stone walls still standing.

Some rusty machinery stood amongst brambles, long metal cylinders and tall iron arms, some bent at an angle. The stream plunged under the path and splashed down the other side of a wall, where it had once turned a water-wheel. Only the hub remained, and one or two wooden spokes.

From here onwards the valley was bare. She reached the ledge over the beach, through which the stream had cut a channel, and looked out to sea. The waves were breaking against the headlands, and the spray hung like smoke over the shore. An island appeared through the mist.

She thought of Mr Treloar coming down the valley, ever since he was a boy all those years ago, watching for the peregrine falcons on the cliffs and the flocks of woodcock coming in from the sea.

As she approached the farm, she heard laughter. She let herself into the kitchen. Everyone except Mrs Treloar was there, the old man in his usual corner, her mother next to him, and Mr and Mrs Rowe at the table. They glanced up as she entered, and then looked back at Nancy, who continued her story.

"So I stopped the car, I thought he wanted a lift into the village. The old man got in and I drove off again. 'You've taken your time!' he said crossly. I was so surprised I said, 'Oh, have I?' He turned and looked at me in amazement. 'Madam, I'm terribly sorry,' he said. 'I was waiting for my son, he drives the same sort of car!'"

Nancy and Vera laughed, but Desmond stared into his cup of tea on the table. Vera Rowe poured a cup for Fran.

"I've got a daughter at your school," she said, as she handed it to her. "Do you know Shirley Rowe?"

"No," said Fran.

"She's in the same year as you," said Nancy.

"There are three hundred in the fifth year," said Fran. "I don't know everybody. I probably know her by sight."

But the name seemed familiar, and when she thought about it she remembered her, a blonde-haired, loud-mouthed girl in another tutor group. The two women went on talking about the size of schools. Desmond drank his tea and kept himself to himself.

Mr Treloar was unable to hear any of this, but he was preparing to join in the conversation. By now Fran recognised the signs, like the whirring of a grandfather clock before it strikes; the gleam in the eyes, the movement of the lips, the way he leaned his head forward.

"Did you see any seals?" he asked her, cutting across the conversation about schools. Each of the 'see' sounds was spoken with great deliberation.

"No," she said.

"It's a wonderful beach for seals," he said. "Did you see the cave?"

She shook her head.

"If you go down at low tide and go round the head-land, you come to a large cave with a sandy beach. The grey seals used this as a nursery for their young. I never knew a year but what they bred there—sometimes only five or six, and one or two years I've seen as many as twenty. It was a marvellous sight at the end of this tunnel looking seaward watching the mother seals coming into the cave on the incoming tide to nurse their young ones."

Fran was thrilled by the old man's description. As he spoke, he no longer saw the room around him, but was back in the cave again, with the sea churning around the entrance and the seals flopping on to the sand.

"If the tide was in I used to go down a mine shaft

which was fitted with ladders, out quite a distance through the old workings of the mine, to a tunnel which led to the shore. I remember once looking out from the cave, and there was a sight I doubt very much was ever seen before or since. There were over seventy full-grown seals lying on the beach."

He paused for them to take it in. "I should say by the smell of their breath, they'd had a big feed of fish out to sea, and came in to sleep it off." He chuckled at the memory.

Mrs Rowe gave a patronising smile. "They love to remember the old days, don't they?" she said.

"Well, we saw another side to him!" said Nancy when they were in the car. "He's certainly got a temper. I bet he was a tyrant when he was young."

"He was in the right though."

"These relatives always go on about what ought to be done, but it's a different matter if they have to do it."

"He'd never go and live with the Rowes."

"It wouldn't work. He doesn't get on with his grandson. He orders him about, and Desmond does exactly what he's told, but all the time he does it as though he hates it."

"He seems to be afraid of the old man."

"He's afraid of not getting his share of the money. It's always money that causes trouble in families. You ought to be glad we haven't got any relatives. I've seen them do the most dreadful things. I went to a little old lady once and she was in terrible pain but her daughters were trying to get a signature out of her. They were shaking her and trying to sit her up and when I wanted to give her an injection they shrieked at me and tried to hold me back—they thought she would never come round."

"Did she?"

"No," said Nancy. "But what a way to go! I told Mrs

Rowe, I expect the relatives to do more. We won't be going in there every day from now on."

"Are you pulling out?"

"No, not completely. We shall keep an eye on them, but they don't need any real nursing care. They can manage for themselves, now that they're on the ground floor. They've agreed to have a home help, and Mrs Bray was able to do a few extra hours, so that's all arranged. With Mavis going in regularly and a little more family involvement, they should be all right. I think really, for all the brave front he put up, Mr Treloar thought they had come to the end. Now they've had a reprieve, and he's full of the joys of life."

"The joys of life!" thought Fran. And yet the expression did not seem too inappropriate.

Two

When the mock exams were over and they had returned to normal work at school, one of her English assignments—out of a choice of subjects—was to interview an old person. Fran immediately thought of Mr Treloar and decided that she would like to interview him. Nancy had not mentioned him for some weeks, so she asked her mother how the old couple were getting on at Penhallow Farm.

"They're coping very well," said Nancy. "He's still as sharp as a razor, but his wife is getting a bit vague. She starts to do things and then forgets what she was doing. She made a pot of tea the last time I was there, and do you think we could find it! I knew she'd made it, because the kettle was hot, the water had been emptied out, and the teapot was missing. We hunted everywhere. And do you know where it was? She'd put it in the oven!"

"That sounds like someone else I know!"

"Come off it, I'm not that bad yet!" She pretended to take a swipe at Fran. "Mr Treloar is very good, he just laughs at it all. He gets a little impatient sometimes . . . Oh, I was cross with the doctor, though. He'd been to see them and took off the old man's socks and shoes—the ones I'd 'mutilated'—to look at his ankles. And he left them off. It was so thoughtless. It takes Mr Treloar ages to get his socks on again, it's a real struggle for him. I got there an hour later and he was worn out. You've got to think of things like that when you're dealing with old people."

"What does he do when he gets up in the morning?"

"My dear, he doesn't get out of them from one week to the next. All the old people sleep in vests, long underpants and socks. If you can get them to have one bath a week you're doing well. Then someone like Rosemary, of course, comes straight out of hospital and expects them to strip off and have a bath every day. She'd kill them with baths."

"Do you think it would be too much if I interviewed him?" She explained about the English assignment.

"He'd love it," said Nancy. "He's always dying to talk to someone, and I just haven't got the time. It would make his day!"

The following afternoon she picked up Fran as soon as she got home, and they drove to Penhallow. A lot of the gorse in the lane was out in flower, though it was not yet in full blossom, and there were primroses under the banks. None of the trees was in leaf but the buds covered them with a pinkish-brown haze, and in the bottom of the valley the willows were white with catkins. The hillsides looked greener, the opposite side of the valley less dark, but down towards the sea the blue and grey stone remained unchanged.

A strong wind was blowing from the south-west and the clouds were racing across the sky. The branches rattled above their heads as they went down the path that Desmond had cleared. In the kitchen Mr and Mrs Treloar sat on either side of the stove, with rugs over their laps.

The old man had a secretive, knowing smile on his face. He drew his hand from under the rug and held it out, concealing something inside the clenched fist.

"Take it!" he said.

"You won't catch me!" said Nancy.

He held it out to Fran.

"What is it?" she asked.

He just sat and smiled. Cautiously she put her hand beneath his, palm upwards, ready to pull away quickly if it was unpleasant.

He opened his fist, and a paw dropped on to her hand. She shrank back a little, but did not drop it. It was furry, brown and white.

"Do you know what that is?" he asked.

"A rabbit's paw?"

"It's a hare's paw . . . And do you know what it's for?"

"Good luck?"

"No," said Mr Treloar.

His wife watched him with a benevolent smile, as though she had seen him produce these things many times before.

"The miners used this to assay tin," he said. "If you wanted to know the percentage of tin in the ore, you'd take a sample and crush it down in a panning shovel, and then you'd brush it with a hare's paw."

He mimed the movement, very delicately brushing away from himself with his thickened fingers.

"The hare's paw would sweep away the lighter stone, and leave the tin in the shovel."

"I didn't know you were a miner," said Nancy. Her voice was always pitched high when she talked to Mr Treloar, and ended with a clear key word. He had no difficulty in understanding her.

"Miner?" he asked, head back and eyes looking fierce. "I was never a miner. I used to look for tin on the cliffs and in the old workings. I'd collect the rock until I had a cartload, and then I'd take it down to the works in the next valley. There it would be assayed, and I would be paid accordingly. I've found some wonderful specimens in my time."

He started to get up, leaning on his frame.

"What do you want?" asked Nancy.

"Pass me that drawer," he commanded, pointing to one of the small drawers in the top row of the dresser.

Fran pulled it open, and it was full of rocks and stones. It was very heavy when she took the full weight; she lifted it on to a chair by his side.

Some looked like ordinary stones, others sparkled in the light; they were black, grey and brown, and some were clear white tinged with orange. He picked up a lump of metal, like cubes fused together, different facets catching the light, and handed it to Nancy. Her hand dropped a little at the unexpected weight.

"Is it silver?" she asked.

"Silver?" he repeated scornfully.

"Oops, sorry!" said Nancy.

"That's mundic."

He searched through the stones and picked out a large, flattish specimen. It was brown, with black lumps in it; it looked like a slice of very stale Christmas cake. He held it out to Fran, who felt its weight. As she turned it in her hand, different lights in it sparkled like frost.

"That's tin," he said, almost with reverence.

"I'll tell you a story about that stone," he went on. "When I was a boy there was an old man who worked on the cliff face. I remember seeing him with a rope round his waist, the other end of the rope tied to a miner's drill driven into the rocks for safety. He knocked off pieces of tin-bearing rock with a hammer and gad, and put them into a bag hanging from his shoulders. His name was Billy Moyle, and he gave me this stone when I was eight years old."

Fran looked at it lying in her hand, and thought how in the last century an old man hanging at the end of a rope had chipped it out of the cliff face. She passed it to her mother.

"Mr Treloar," said Nancy, "Frances would like to interview you."

"Interview?" he said, jerking his head up and drawing his brows together so that the two deep lines appeared in his forehead.

"It's her work for school," said Nancy. "She'd like to ask you some questions."

"What does she want to know?"

"She wants to know about you."

"About me?" He looked across at his wife, whose eyes were closed, her head nodding. "Why does she want to know about me?"

"Because you've lived a long life and you've seen a lot of changes."

"I have," he agreed.

"You tell Fran about them, while I go and see another patient." She got up to go. "I'll come back and pick you up in about an hour," she said to Fran.

"But . . . I thought you were going to stay."

"I'm supposed to be working."

"I thought you'd put the questions, he never understands me."

"Go on, you'll be all right!" said Nancy. "Speak into his left ear, like I do . . . I'll see you later."

She was gone, and the only sounds in the room were the drawn-in breaths of Mr Treloar, the gentle snoring of his wife, and the ticking of the grandfather clock in the hall. The wind sighed in the trees above the farm.

Fran returned the drawer of mineral specimens to the dresser, and sat on the chair. She leaned towards the old man, closer than she would normally speak to anyone; she felt uneasy and a little repelled by the closeness. She could smell his body and his clothes. It was not unpleasant, nor pleasant neither: a sort of soapy smell, with a slight sourness underneath it.

"Mr Treloar," she said, "where were you born?"

"Eh?" he asked. He had turned the side of his face towards her, and now darted his head round to look at her.

61

She wished her mother had been there as interpreter. She tried to imitate her way of emphasising the last word.

"Where were you *born*?"

To her relief, he understood. "I was born in this house."

"How long ago?"

"Eighty-nine years ago, I shall be ninety next birthday," he said. "My father was a tenant farmer, just as his father before him. And then when I was a boy the squire had to sell some of his property, and my father bought the farm."

Fran scribbled down as much as she could in the notebook on her lap. Once he had started, Mr Treloar did not need much prompting. He described how he left school at fourteen, to start work on the farm. The boys with fathers and brothers who were miners left at an earlier age, to go into the mines. A farm-lad was paid five shillings a week, and worked from seven to five, six days a week and every other Sunday morning.

He turned towards the dresser. "Open that long drawer!" he ordered. In the middle drawer of the dresser she found what he was looking for, several photograph albums. They had padded brown covers, and were held together with faded gold braid. She opened one; the pages were interleaved with tissue paper which had a spider's web design, and through the web the fading brown photographs showed dimly. She turned over the tissue.

The photos recorded the life of the farm, and he spoke as though it was all still fresh in his mind. He pointed out a brown photograph labelled in white ink, 'Croust at hay-making'. It showed a large hay-mow with a party of workers sitting beneath it, the men in shirt sleeves and the women in sun bonnets. The sun shone into their eyes, and they squinted at the camera. In front of them were baskets and ewers.

"What's croust?" Fran asked.

"Croust?" he questioned. "Why, it's the food a miner takes down the mine, or a farmer eats in the fields. Our croust was always a saffron bun about the size of a dinner plate, and hot milky coffee."

He passed the album to his wife, who woke up.

"That's at Trengoose," she said.

"Of course it's not!" he shouted. "It's at Penhallow!"

"Oh yes," she said.

Fran looked at photos of threshing machines and traction engines, horses and cows, the farm under snow.

"That was the shooting house," he said, pointing to a building with long icicles hanging from the roof.

Fran thought it was a sort of slaughterhouse. "What did you shoot?" she asked.

He laughed, very pleased with her slightly shocked reaction. "It's where we put the potatoes to sprout—the shooting house!"

She glanced up at him, and saw that he had said it to tease her. She smiled at the old-fashioned joke.

They were still looking at the albums when Nancy returned.

"You can't come back yet!" said Mr Treloar. "I've only just begun!"

But Nancy rushed immediately across the kitchen to Mrs Treloar. "Look at her!" she exclaimed. "Couldn't you see her!"

Fran looked across at the old lady; she was sitting slumped sideways in her chair, with her eyes closed and her mouth gaping.

"I thought she was asleep," said the old man.

"She's not asleep," said Nancy. "She's unconscious."

They lifted her, Nancy on one side and Fran on the other, and carried her into the bedroom. She opened her eyes, but stared vacantly as though she could not see anyone. She wanted to say something, but was unable to speak.

Nancy put a pillow under her head and eased her clothing. "Fran, will you go up to the car and fetch some paper sheets. They're on the back seat. Here, take the keys!" She threw them to her, and as Fran left she heard her reassuring Mr Treloar. "Yes, she'll be all right. Look, she's come round already."

Fran hurried up the lane, without running, glad to be outside. Her hand was wet, where she had supported the old lady from underneath. She trailed it through a patch of fresh grass on top of the bank.

When she returned, her mother had got Mrs Treloar into bed. She took the sheets and started packing them under and around the old lady.

"What are you doing to me?" she complained.

"I'm just making you comfortable."

"Who are you?"

"That's Nurse!" said Mr Treloar. "Don't you know Nurse?"

"Don't speak to her crossly," said Nancy. "Just sit by the bed and hold her hand."

"She doesn't know me."

"Keep talking to her, she soon will."

As they went out, they could hear the voice of the old man: "Don't you know me, Lettie? This is Tom, your husband. You're at Penhallow." Fran closed the door, and the voice continued as a distant rumbling.

Nancy picked up the phone. "I'll stay until the doctor comes," she said. "What will you do?"

"I'll walk home," said Fran. She would only feel in the way if she remained.

She walked along the road, her head down against the wind, seeing little of her surroundings. She felt guilty. The interview had gone well and she had enjoyed talking to Mr Treloar, and then suddenly everything had changed.

She had not even noticed that the old lady was ill. And even if she had, she would not have been able to help her. She always wanted to run away from illness or anything unpleasant.

She could not help it, it was the way she was. Not everyone could be like her mother. Nancy was used to it, she was trained and knew what to do.

And yet she still blamed herself. She had never had anything to do with her mother's patients in the past, except to take telephone messages. She should never have gone back for the interview. She would keep away in future. She would not get involved, it was too upsetting.

She was writing up the interview when Nancy came home.

"How is she?" Fran asked.

"Not bad," said Nancy. "She recognises you now, but she still thinks she's at Trengoose. Mr Treloar says it's the farm she was brought up on."

"What happened to her?"

"She had another CVA."

"What's that?"

"A cerebral vascular accident," said Nancy. "A black-out, a slight stroke."

"What does it do?"

"It's a clot of blood which interferes with the function of the brain. Sometimes you can't speak after a stroke, it depends which side of the brain is affected. I've got one stroke who can only say no. When she was in hospital the orderlies would come along and say, 'Would you like a cup of tea, dear?' and she would be dying for a drink but when she tried to say 'yes' it came out as 'no', and on they went. It was very bad nursing, she should have been on a liquids chart. When she came out of hospital, I asked her what it was like to be home, and she managed to say

65

'Gosh! Lovely—lovely—lovely.' But Mrs Treloar got her speech back very quickly. It's left her weak down one side, but that might improve."

"She looked dreadful," said Fran. She could still see her slumped in the chair, her mouth wide open.

"Mr Treloar sent you a message," said Nancy. "He said he's got a lot more to tell you."

"I don't need any more."

"Well, he hopes you'll go and see him again."

"I've got a lot of work," said Fran.

But over the next two weeks she was continually reminded of him.

"He keeps on, every time I go there," said Nancy. "'When's the maid coming down? I've thought of a lot more things to tell her.'"

"I've handed the writing in."

"I know, I tell him that. But he doesn't seem to understand. He keeps telling me stories to pass on to you, he was telling me today how to make a hand-mow. He always manages to think of something just as I'm going."

And then one day Nancy handed her a pale blue envelope when she came back from school. Fran turned it over; there was no writing on either side.

"What is it?" she asked.

"Open it and see."

She picked up a knife from the table and slit it open. She took out a note, with just the address, Penhallow Farm, at the top.

"It's from Mr Treloar," she said.

The writing was large, with big loops to the letters; it looked as though it had been written with a dip-pen. It was a bit shaky.

> 'I thought you might like to know that this farm was the last place where the Cornish chough was seen in the district . . .' she read.

66

It must have been a great effort for him to write it with his arthritic fingers. She could imagine them holding the pen, forcing it into the shape of the letters, slowly and deliberately crossing the page.

"You ought to go and see him," said Nancy. "It means so much to him."

"All right," said Fran. "I'll go in the Easter holidays."

Nancy drove her to the farm one bright and windy spring day. There were patches of purple on the blue-green sea, and the horizon made a clear, sharp line against the sky; the gorse in the lane was a blaze of yellow.

The old couple were sitting as usual in the kitchen, on either side of the stove. Fran glanced, a little cautiously, at Mrs Treloar. She knew that because of her incontinence, she now had a catheter, but there were no signs of plastic tubes and urine bags. She looked as she always had, white-haired and red-cheeked, a vague smile on her lips. She sat slightly lopsided in the chair; Nancy went across and straightened her up, and asked her how she was.

"I'm all right," she said.

"She sleeps all the time," said Mr Treloar.

"I've been talking to Frank Pascoe about you," said Nancy, turning to the old man.

He pressed his lips into a firm line, as he always did at the mention of Frank Pascoe. It was almost a game between him and Nancy.

"I asked him if he remembered you. He said whenever he saw you, you were on the beach or on the cliffs. He said you were a wrecker."

"We used to call it wrecking," he said, "but it was what you would nowadays call beachcombing."

"So you weren't on the cliffs with lights, trying to lure the ships on to the rocks."

"No!" he said fiercely. "That's an injustice to the

Cornish, they've never done that. They always saved the lives of seafarers first, but after that they regarded anything that was washed up as theirs."

Fran saw that the old lady was sitting in a wheel-chair, and she held the doors open while Nancy took her into the bedroom. Then she sat down by the side of the old man. "What did you find on the beach?" she asked.

"The first I remember was a lot of candles being washed up." He settled back into his chair. "Now, those candles came exactly the right time for the people living round about, not many at that time possessing an oil-lamp. Some of the candles were in full boxes, but most came in loose and were broken up a bit. They could be picked up by the sackful."

Fran thought of what was washed ashore now; the high-water mark was always a litter of lumps of tar and oil, plastic bottles and containers, nothing but rubbish. She would have enjoyed searching the beaches for valuable salvage.

"When the First World War broke out, all kinds of articles began to come ashore. The wreckage had to be seen to be believed! Butter, lard and bacon, all undamaged by the sea-water. At one time there was a large number of barrels of brandy, which had to be drawn out in cans. It took ten trips up the cliff to drain each one, and another trip for the empty barrel."

Fran could feel how much he had enjoyed wrecking. She could imagine him on a stormy night, running into the waves to hold on to the planks that were being swept out, struggling in moonlight up a narrow cliff-path, carrying an empty barrel on his back. Farming had been his work, but wrecking and tinning had been his excitement. They were like hunting for treasure, never knowing what wealth you might suddenly find.

Nancy wheeled Mrs Treloar back into the kitchen. She said that she would go and do Mrs Chynoweth and call back later. Fran was left alone with the old couple, and for a while they sat without talking. It was an easy silence; with anyone else she would have felt awkward. But Mr Treloar was thinking about the past and Mrs Treloar was lost in her own memories; there was no need to say anything. She absorbed the sounds of the house and the outside world. She could hear the distant sound of the sea.

"I've kept a few things which have come off wrecks," Mr Treloar said after a while. "Many years ago a small sailing vessel was caught in the bay. I watched her all one Sunday going to and fro, trying to stand out to sea, and all the time being driven closer to the shore. At last she struck the headland, and a big wave swept her off and drove her right into the cove. By the next morning's tide she had gone all to pieces . . . She had her name, *Bona Fortuna*, across the stern in brass letters, and I got one off but I wanted the T, for my name—Thomas Treloar. There was one screw left. I was soaked to the skin, but I was determined to get this T. It nearly cost me my life, and I didn't get it in the end."

He started to stand up, leaning on his frame, then changed his mind. "Reach up on top of the dresser," he said.

Fran could easily feel over the lip round the top, and felt amongst the dust and grime a flat metal object. She took it down: it was a brass letter F, about a foot high.

"What's your name?" he asked.

"Frances."

"I thought that was a boy's name."

"It's spelt differently."

He took it and started cleaning off the dust with the rug over his knees. "I reckon it was meant for you," he said. "I should like you to have it."

"Oh no, I couldn't!" said Fran. It was completely unexpected, she was quite taken aback.

"Why not?"

"Well, it's yours. You took it off the boat, it means something to you."

"It's no good to me now."

He pressed it into her hands, and she tried to push it back on to his lap. But he was very determined, and began to look angry. She left the brass letter on the table and fetched metal polish and a rag from the scullery. Then she set to and rubbed and polished until it shone like gold.

It was the first thing that Nancy noticed when she came back.

"What's that?" she asked.

"I took that off a wreck," said Mr Treloar. "I want the maid to have it."

"You can't do that!" said Nancy.

His mouth began to work, and his hands moved in agitation. "I want the maid to have it," he repeated sharply.

Fran looked uncomfortably from the old man to her mother. She would have liked to keep the initial, but she would rather it had never been offered than have a scene over it.

"It's a very kind thought," said Nancy. "But you mustn't give your things away."

"I will not be treated like a child!" the old man fumed. "If I want to give something away, I'll give it away. I've given the letter to the maid." He sat back as though the matter was finished.

"Have you accepted it?" Nancy asked Fran.

"No," said Fran. But somehow polishing it seemed more of an acceptance than saying yes. "I don't know."

"Do you want it?"

"Yes." She would have liked to accept it. There was the coincidence of it being her initial, and she thought of Mr Treloar snatching it from the sea as the waves

70

pounded the wreck, breaking over him and nearly drowning him.

"But you shouldn't do it, you know!" Nancy scolded.

"If that grandson of mine got hold of it, he'd sell it for scrap!" said the old man.

There was an unusual silence in the car; Nancy and Fran very rarely quarrelled. Fran held the brass letter in her lap, and felt uncomfortable about it.

"Why didn't you want me to take it?" she asked.

"I never accept anything from patients," said Nancy. "I make that a rule."

"Not even Black Magic chocolates?"

"They're always from relatives, not from patients. You know you won't be seeing them again. Then you aren't under any obligation."

"He wasn't trying to do that!"

"I don't know. A lot of old people have to use their money or possessions to buy friendship."

"I wouldn't go to see him just for what I could get out of him," said Fran.

"I know you wouldn't. So it's best not to take anything and then it can't look as though you go for the wrong motive."

"You can take it back if you like."

Nancy laughed. "My dear, that's more than my life's worth. He can't bear anyone to cross him, can he? You'd better keep it now."

"I'm not that bothered about it."

"I get offered all sorts of things," said Nancy. She always forgot differences very quickly, and was already quite herself again. "There's one old man I go to once a month. I give him an injection and then he says, 'Now, Nurse, I know the proper thing to do,' and he reaches in his pocket and takes out a 10p piece. I always treat it very seriously. 'Oh, Mr Nankivel,' I say, 'I'm not allowed to

71

accept money.' And he quickly puts it back in his pocket before I can change my mind."

Fran felt the brass initial lying heavy on her lap, cold against her fingers. She did not want him to think that he had to pay her to go and see him. She felt a bit like a modern wrecker coming away with her booty.

Every day that Nancy went to the farm, she brought back a message from Tom Treloar. When was the maid coming again? He had more stories to tell her about wrecking. He wanted to read what she had written about him.

So one afternoon about a week later, when she was still on holiday, Fran went to Penhallow again. As before, Nancy took her when she called to see Mrs Treloar, and would collect her on her way back from visiting other patients. It was raining, and they hurried down the lane, heads bent against the shower. Large drops splashed out of the trees, and the wet undergrowth soaked their legs by the time they reached the house.

There was an array of brass objects on the kitchen table, a ship's compass and other nautical instruments. Nancy very deliberately ignored them, and wheeled the old lady into the bedroom. Fran gave her piece of writing to Mr Treloar, and sat and waited while he read it.

He leaned forward in his chair, holding the sheets of paper to the light. He read without glasses, but frowned with concentration. He took a long time and Fran wondered if he had fallen asleep, but then he turned over the page and continued in the same way. She felt that her words had never been scrutinised so thoroughly.

She wondered what he did all day, now that he no longer had to spend so much time preparing meals and keeping the stove alight. He must spend hours just sitting, with no one to talk to, for his wife was not much company.

72

When he had finished, he looked up at her, his chin pulled back into his neck. "That's very good," he said decisively. " 'Tis proper writing."

"Do you like reading?" she asked.

"I've read every book in this house two or three times," he said. "I'm reading *Pilgrim's Progress* again."

"Would you like me to get some library books for you?"

He did not understand at first, and she had to repeat the question.

"I should like that very much," he said.

"What sort of books?"

He thought about it for a while. "Books about mining," he said, "and about how people used to live and about old Cornwall."

"I'll bring you some," said Fran. The local sections of the school library and the container van which came to the village twice a week were full of books which he would enjoy. She looked forward to picking out the right ones for him.

"I've been thinking about my memories, and all the things I know about the old days that will be forgotten when I'm gone. I'd like you to write them all down for me."

"I couldn't do that!" said Fran quickly.

"I'd pay you for your time."

He always seemed to think that everyone had to be paid, and that if you paid you could get anything. "It's not a question of money," said Fran. "I couldn't do it. I'm not able to."

"You write very well."

"I haven't got the time."

He looked disappointed. Fran felt mean, but she could not possibly commit herself to his plan. "I've got my exams," she said.

"Would you be able to do it when the exams are finished?"

73

"I'll see," she said. He was very persistent.

"Only I haven't got much time left."

"What's this?" exclaimed Nancy, aggressively cheerful as she came back with Mrs Treloar. "Who's talking about not having much time left?"

"I've looked out some more things I've got by wrecking," he said, when Nancy had gone. On the table the brass instruments gleamed dully, some tinged with a greenish-grey.

Fran eyed them doubtfully.

"Do you know what that is?" he asked. He pointed to a large screw-shaped object, and she passed it to him. It went with a brass dial; there was a pointer on the front and lots of cog-wheels inside, all made of the same metal. He waited for a reply.

"I don't know," she said. It looked a bit like a propeller.

"It's a ship's log," said Mr Treloar. "This part trailed in the water and turned a line which was attached to these cog-wheels, which registered the speed." He demonstrated all the moving parts, taking pleasure in the weighty metal. "I took it off the *Bona Fortuna*," he said, "so it goes with the letter from the name. I want you to take it."

"No!" exclaimed Fran, almost before he had finished.

"I'm giving it to you."

But she moved away before he could put it into her hands, and stood by the side of Mrs Treloar.

"Take it, dear," said the old lady. "He always gets his own way in the end."

"I'm not taking it," she said. "I don't come here just for what I can get!"

"I can't hear you," shouted Mr Treloar.

He looked thunderous, as he always did when he was thwarted. His wife smiled benevolently. Fran approached

74

him cautiously, and leaned over towards the left side of his head. "I don't come for what I can get, I come to see *you*," she shouted.

"Hmm!" He thought about this for a while. She wondered if he was working himself into a fury; if he made a scene she would never come back again. But when at last he spoke, it was quite quietly. "I'm not used to anyone doing anything for nothing," he said. "I only see my relatives when they want something out of me. I gave Desmond fifty pounds for moving the bedroom downstairs. I saw young Alec, my sister's grandson, last week, the first time for months. He had written off his car in an accident, and wanted to buy a new one. He expected me to help him. I reckon you and your mother are the only people who don't ask me for anything."

She had refused payment. Fran felt that she had stood up to him.

"Now, when are we going to get on with the writing?" he asked.

"I'll try and see you once a week," she said. "But I don't promise."

"What about next Monday?"

"I shall be back at school."

"In the evening."

"I'll come *one* evening."

As they moved their heads apart, they exchanged glances. There was a glint in his eyes, a look of triumph at having got what he wanted.

"What was he saying to you about not having much time left?" asked Nancy. They had returned home, and were eating their evening meal.

"He wants me to write down his memories for him."

"You've got your school work to do."

"That's what I said."

"He was trying to make you feel sorry for him. They

all try it. 'It's time I was gone, I've out-lived my useful-ness.' That's the usual cry."

"He didn't say that. There's still something he wants to do."

"As long as he doesn't take too much of your time, that's all."

Fran thought there was something different in Nancy's attitude. "Have you turned against him?" she asked.

"No, I think he's a remarkable old man. I think it's marvellous to have something you want to achieve at ninety, and to be planning for it."

"You've become hostile towards him, though."

"I just don't want you to neglect your work. And if you aren't careful he'd persuade you to. He's like an old fox, he knows all the tricks. He'll try anything, bribery, flattery, pity, anger. He knows how to play them all. I went to one old man this morning and he said, 'Nurse, I need someone to take an interest in me.' That's what they all need, though no one's going to take an interest in poor old Mr Hicks. But Mr Treloar knows how to make himself interesting. He can get his own way, even at ninety. There's no need to feel sorry for him, he doesn't need it."

Fran was not very keen on writing down everything from his dictation. She did enough note-taking at school, and her homework was nearly always writing. Nancy suggested that she could record his memories on tape, and she took her cassette recorder the next time she went to the farm.

She waited until her mother had left, and then lifted the recorder out of her bag, without giving any explanation of what it was. It was still inside its original box. She removed the lid. Mr Treloar leaned forward, keenly in-terested in the contents.

Previously he had always prepared something to show

Fran; now she had brought something to show him, and she adopted his manner of making a bit of a mystery of it.

"What do you think that is?" she asked, as she took the machine out of its box, and placed the lead and microphone on the table.

"It's one of those tape-recorders," said the old man.

"It's a cassette recorder," said Fran. "I'm going to record your voice."

He was always fascinated by things and how they worked, whether it was a horse-drawn mower his father had bought in the last century, or a Japanese cassette recorder of the present day. Fran showed him the cassette, and how it slotted in. Then she fitted the microphone, and plugged in the lead, using an adaptor that she had brought in her bag.

She handed him the microphone and showed him how to switch on when he was ready to speak. She pressed down the RECORD button.

He tried to get used to the feel of the microphone, and held it towards himself. Fran raised it closer to his lips. He treated it very seriously. There was something—not funny, not incongruous, almost touching—about this very old man holding a microphone to his lips in the manner of a disc jockey or a television reporter.

"Tell me the story you told the other day, about the wreckers," said Fran.

Very deliberately, he pressed the switch and spoke into the microphone. "There were two young men who found a mast on the beach . . ."

It did not sound right. When he told the story before, it sounded so natural. Now it was stilted and artificial.

After a moment or two, he switched off with an exasperated jerk of the microphone. "I can't get used to the dang thing!" he exclaimed.

"You're making it different," said Fran. "Tell it as you did last time."

77

"I can't talk Cornish into it."

"Why not?"

"If it's recorded, it's got to be proper English."

"It hasn't," said Fran. "Just speak as you usually do."

"When I was a boy . . ." he began. He had not switched the microphone on. He started again. "When I was a lad . . ." He stopped again.

"Have a rest," said Fran.

"No, I will not be beaten!" he said emphatically. "I shall master the dang thing yet!"

He had not switched off, so she ran the tape back and played what he had said. His sentences rang out again in the room, in a slightly thinner version.

He looked up with startled eyes. "That's not me!" he said. "I don't sound like that!"

"That's you!" said Fran.

"Well! I didn't know I was so Cornish. It sounded more like Frank Pascoe to me—downright ignorant!"

Mrs Treloar started to laugh. He glared at his wife, then turned back to Fran.

"This time we're going to do it," he said. He stared fixedly at her. "Right, switch on!"

"How was that?" he asked as soon as he had finished.

"Very good!"

She played it back to the old couple, and he listened, a little bit suspiciously at first, and then with enjoyment.

It told the story of how as a boy very early one morning he had found a mast washed up on the shore. He struggled to get it above the high-water mark, and then went off to fetch help. Meanwhile a naval man claimed it, and went shares in it with a farmer who hitched it to a cart and dragged it further up the beach. So that night he took a cross-cut saw, cut the spar into four lengths, and buried them in a trench in the sand. When the men found that it had gone, each accused the other of taking it.

Twelve months later young Tom dug out the lengths and sold them to a cabinet maker.

Mr Treloar laughed at the end, as though it was someone else's story and he had heard it for the first time. He seemed able to hear the tape without any difficulty.

Fran, too, wanted it to be a good recording and listened attentively. She was quite pleased with the result.

"Let's do another one," he said eagerly.

They played it back. There were fewer pauses and hesitations than in the first tape. All his stories, Fran thought, were about battles of wit: boys outwitting men, wreckers outwitting coast-watchers. Even the struggle to earn a living from the land or the sea or under the ground was a fight to outwit the elements. You had to be cunning to survive.

Fran was ready for a break, but once he had got into the swing of it he wanted to go on. In the middle of his third story, the stop button on the recorder jumped up with a loud ping.

"What's that?" he asked.

"It's the end of the tape."

"Is that all we can do?" He sounded disappointed.

"I can turn it over and use the other side."

"How much does a tape cost?" he asked. He reached into his jacket pocket and took out his wallet. It was stuffed full of notes. "I want to pay for it."

"That's all right," said Fran. "It's a spare one, you can have it."

"What do you mean?"

"It's a present," she said.

"Present?" he repeated. He looked surprised, and thought about it for a while. "We shall need some more," he said. "I'll give you the money, and you can buy them for me."

Fran hesitated. But there could be nothing wrong with

it, she was only running an errand for him. "All right," she said.

"Would this be enough?" he asked, holding out a five pound note.

"I'll buy two and give you the change."

He waved his hand as though he did not want to hear about the change. She took the note and put it into her purse in the bag. She felt a little uneasy handling it; she would rather not be involved with anything to do with money, but it was what he wanted and it was not for her.

They finished the story on the other side of the tape. He wanted to continue, but she said it was enough for one day. "You can have the recorder if you like, and tape on your own."

He shook his head. "I can't do it on my own."

"You can," said Fran. "You know how to work it."

"I can't do it unless you're there," he said.

"But that doesn't make any difference."

"I need you to talk to," he said simply. He looked her straight in the eyes, until she glanced away.

The following week, Nancy went to work in a neighbouring district. One of the nurses there was on holiday, and the other had become ill. Rosemary was left to look after Stennack, and Nancy travelled each day some miles along the coast to a seaside resort. There were many more retired people there, and she always referred to it as the Costa Geriatrica.

She came home exhausted each day. "They've got a different attitude to you over there," she said. "They'd treat you like a servant, if you let them. They'd expect you to arrive when it suited them. 'Why are you so late?' said one woman, very snooty. 'I'll tell you why I'm so late,' I said. 'I'm late because I've been with a little old lady who had a heavy stroke and I thought your tiny ulcer could wait a while!' One military type started talking politics. I put up with it for so long, and then I said, 'And which party started the Health Service, Major Flint? If it wasn't for them you'd have to pay for all these expensive dressings I'm putting on your leg.' He didn't say anything after that . . . The trouble is, I don't know where anywhere is. All I've got is a name and address, I don't even know what I'm expected to do when I get there. I went to one house and this tiny little woman came to the door, almost a dwarf, but very jolly hockey-sticks in manner. 'Do come in, my dear!' And then this tiny little man came out of one of the rooms. He was absolutely senile. 'What do I have to do for you?' I asked. 'I don't know,' he said. His sister had disappeared. 'Well, let's go into the bathroom and see what happens,' I said, hoping he'd know the routine. He just stood there. 'What does the nurse usually do?' I asked. 'I don't know,' he said. 'Well, sit down!' I said. And he sat down on the floor. Then he couldn't get up! 'Do you think I could go for a bicycle ride today?' he asked. 'When did you last go for a bicycle ride?' 'About twenty years ago,' he said."

Fran put off visiting the farm until her mother was working in her own district again. She went into the town one lunch time and bought two ninety-minute cassettes with Mr Treloar's money, and thought that she would take them to him at the weekend, when they could continue recording. But as it happened her plans had to be changed.

On the Wednesday evening she was reading in the sitting-room. Nancy had been on the phone, it seemed for hours. When she came in, she said, "Well, your mate's in hospital."

"Who's that?"

"Mr Treloar and his wife, they've both been taken into Goonlaze House."

"Oh no!" said Fran.

She had somehow imagined that the crisis was over, and that they would go along for ages as they were, and that she would be visiting them from time to time for as long as she could foresee. Mr Treloar feared Goonlaze House, the Union as he called it, the old Workhouse; it was the worst thing that could have happened to him.

"He had a fall," said Nancy. "They couldn't possibly stay there on their own, so they were both admitted . . . I wish I hadn't been on the other district, I'm sure I could have persuaded him to go without any fuss. There was a terrible scene apparently. He refused to leave the house, and Rosemary, of course, never uses any tact. He was shouting that he wouldn't go, and she said that he'd have to, instead of trying to bring him round to the idea. You can always get him to see reason if you go about it the right way. But she threatened him, told him the doctors would have nothing more to do with him if he didn't go, they'd get a magistrate's order. It just put his back up."

Fran could imagine the scene, the old man shaken by his fall, the young nurse, tight-lipped and righteous, the old lady confused by what was going on. He was always angry if he could not get his own way over even the smallest things, and staying in his own home was what mattered most to him. He would have fought like a trapped animal.

"Wasn't there any way he could have stayed?" she asked.

"How could he?" said Nancy. "They're both bed-ridden, and there's no one to look after them. He reckoned he could still get around, the fall was nothing. He said he'd broken his arm once and he'd never had a doctor, he just strapped it up and it mended itself. Then he remembered a distant relative, a second or third cousin, who had been a nurse. He said she'd come and look after them. 'What makes you think she'd give up her home and her job and everything else to come and look after you?' Rosemary asked him. It turned out that she's over seventy! He's quite convinced that she'll come running the moment he wants her, and he wrote her a letter while they were waiting for the ambulance. The first driver refused to go down the lane and went back to the depot. They had to find a crew who were willing to do it, and it took them ages to get the stretchers up the path from the house."

Frances felt all the indignity and distress of the scene. It was dreadful for him to leave his home like this; after living in it for ninety years, to be carried out by a reluctant ambulance crew, jolted on a stretcher, with no one there that he could trust, only a nurse he blamed for it all and two strangers in blue uniforms. He wouldn't have had a chance to look back at the farm that he was leaving, perhaps for the last time. It was like taking cattle to market.

"Poor old fellow!" said Nancy. "But there wasn't anything else they could do. And I'll say this for Rosemary. She knows what has to be done, and she'll stick to it. He said he'd never speak to her again."

They drove through the lodge gates, and along a drive bordered by rhododendron bushes beneath trees, much taller here than those swept by the salt winds of the north coast. A crowd of signs and white arrows on the tarmac of the road directed them to the car park, some way from the house. Nancy ignored them all and drove right on to the main entrance, swinging the wheel and stopping the car beneath a notice on a wall which said CONSULTANTS ONLY.

"There won't be any at this time of day," she said, in answer to Fran's unspoken question. "They'll be out having a last round of golf."

Other evening visitors were walking up from the car park, some with bunches of daffodils in their hands. On one side of the courtyard was the grey-brick Victorian workhouse. It was three storeys high, with small, arched windows; those on the ground floor were high up and barred.

The entrance was modern, and all glass, and joined to another modern, low building on the other side. They went through two pairs of swing doors into a corridor. There was a large flower arrangement of yellow forsythia and daffodils on a table, and rows of wheel-chairs.

Fran followed her mother into the old building and up a flight of stairs; there were metal grips on the edge of each tread, and a hand-rail against the wall. Everywhere was painted cream and green. They came to a corridor where the edges of the floor curved up to join the walls; it looked as though it was frequently swabbed, and the smell of disinfectant was strong. The swing doors were scarred where wheel-chairs and trolleys scraped against them.

They reached the ward sister's office. Inside was a male nurse in a white overall buttoned up to the neck, with his name on a lapel badge. He wore gold-rimmed glasses and had red hair. He directed them into the ward.

Fran had not known what to expect. As she walked down the ward, looking from left to right, she passed bed after bed, each with an old man lying in it. A few had visitors, who seemed to sit around their relatives, not knowing what to say or holding painful, shouted conversations. The others stared vacantly ahead of them, their mouths drooping. Some were asleep, and were muttering and groaning. One shouted out incoherently as they passed; his cry sounded so urgent and desperate.

Nancy went across to him and listened to the wild sounds he made, while Fran stood at the foot of his bed.

"He's probably like it all the time," said Nancy. "But I'll just tell the charge nurse."

She went back down the ward, and Fran was left on her own in the middle. The old man was staring at her, gabbling broken words. He managed painfully to raise a hand and beckon to her. She felt ill at ease, afraid to go to him in case he grabbed hold of her. She looked towards the door to see if Nancy was coming back.

The ward filled her with horror. Was this what everyone came to? It was a dumping ground for the old and infirm, the decayed and useless. It was all so clean and orderly, with spotless bed-linen and neat lockers; only the ravaged faces of the old men with their empty eyes, their white or time-stained skin and toothless mouths seemed out of place.

Then Nancy and the charge nurse came through the door, laughing together as though they were old friends. The nurse reached out his arm to the old man; the sleeve of his white overall slid above a tattoo-mark on his forearm. He took the old man's hand and spoke to him.

Fran and her mother walked on down the ward, between the rows of the old who could no longer look after themselves, or had no one else to do it for them. She could not bear to think of Mr Treloar being reduced to their level. She was afraid to see him again.

At the end of the ward they turned into a smaller room at the side. Straight ahead of them was Tom Treloar, sitting up in his bed. He saw them at once, his eyes lit up, and he let out a great shout.

"'Tis you, me 'andsome!" he called, as Nancy went up and gave him a kiss.

Fran fetched two stacking chairs and placed one on each side of the bed. Nancy sat on his good side.

"You're looking well!" she said. It was true, he was looking marvellously well. He sat up high in the bed, his pyjamas open at the neck. His face was ruddy, and his eyes lively and bright. He did not look at all like the wrecks in the other ward.

"'Ere, I'm some glad to see 'ee," he said. He spoke with more of an accent in his excitement. "I've got some things to tell 'ee, but before I say anything else I want you to know what a wonderful place this is. It's amazing what they do for you, nothing's too much trouble."

"What's the food like?" asked Nancy.

"The food?" he repeated in his sharp manner. "It's like a first class hotel!"

"Have they given you a pasty?"

"No, not yet," he said, looking at her out of the corner of his eyes, knowing that she was teasing. "But we have a fried breakfast."

At home Mr Treloar always got up at six o'clock and made a bowl of bread and milk, then at nine he ate bacon, liver, sausages and eggs. Once a week he made a huge pasty, containing a pound and a half of best steak.

"I should like the maid to write down a letter to the local papers. I want to tell all the old folk who are worried about going in to Goonlaze House that they have nothing to fear. I can't speak too highly of it."

Fran thought that if she ever found herself in a place like this, she would curl up and die. But he was completely undiminished by it.

"I've met people here I haven't seen for seventy years. In the other ward there are two men who were at school with me. We've had some wonderful talks."

"And how's Lettie?"

"Famous! Every morning they take her down to do gymnastics!" He chuckled at the thought. "They take me down, too, in the lift, to encourage her. 'Come on, Lettie! You can do it!' I say. She'll be walking again soon."

"So Rosemary did the right thing," said Nancy, rather tartly.

His face clouded over, and he pressed his lips together. "I'm not saying that," he said, unforgivingly. "But if

Mrs Treloar gets on her feet again, we shall be able to go home."

"She won't be able to look after you."

"I'm still waiting to hear from Cousin Win."

Nancy raised her eyebrows.

"There's only one thing on my mind now," he said. "And if I could settle that everything would be fine. Could you do a favour for me? I'd like you to go to Penhallow and fetch my address book from the telephone table."

"Why don't you ask Desmond?"

He drew his brows together. "I don't want *him* rummaging through my personal belongings," he said.

"All right," said Nancy. "But I want your signature, I've got to cover myself. I can't just go walking into patients' empty houses."

Fran thought that she was being unnecessarily fussy, but she wrote out the authorisation on the paper her mother produced, and Mr Treloar sat up in bed and signed it. He wrote laboriously, slowly tracing each letter in his large, rounded hand; the old-fashioned T looked more like a J.

He finished his signature, completing it with a flourish. "It's made me think, coming into hospital like this," he said. "I reckon it's time we made our wills. Could you get a solicitor to come and visit me?"

"I think there's someone in the hospital who can make all the arrangements," said Nancy. "I'll go and find out, and I'll see Lettie at the same time."

She went off, and Mr Treloar talked to Fran about the marvels of the hospital. He was keenly interested in the way it was run, the different jobs that people had, the machinery it contained. Suddenly his face changed, and he fell silent. Turning towards the entrance, Fran saw Desmond and his wife Vera approaching the bed.

They both kissed the old man, and sat down on the

87

opposite side. They had been with Mrs Treloar when Nancy arrived. Mr Treloar scowled, and worked his jaws from side to side; he said nothing. They sat in silence until Nancy returned.

"Lettie's complaining that she hasn't seen her husband for months, and he spent all afternoon with her!" she said, when she came back. "She's more confused than ever — though she's much better physically."

"How do you think Grandad is?" asked Mrs Rowe, speaking away from the old man so that he would not be able to hear.

"He's not being very realistic at the moment," said Nancy. "He thinks he'll be going home in a day or two. He's got to accept that he'll be here for a month, and then it won't be easy to go back to looking after themselves."

"Won't they be able to stay here?"

"No, this isn't a long-stay ward. They're here to be rehabilitated."

She leaned over Mr Treloar and spoke close to his ear. "The social worker will see you at ten o'clock tomorrow. He won't see you in the ward, he'll take you to a little room where you'll be private."

She began to gather up her coat and handbag, preparing to go.

Mr Treloar looked triumphantly round at his visitors, and grinned. "I've got the lawyer coming tomorrow," he announced.

Mr and Mrs Rowe jerked up, as though pulled by strings. They glanced nervously at one another. Nancy and Fran left, promising to come again soon.

"He's naughty!" said Nancy on the stairs. "I thought he'd keep quiet about it."

"He really enjoyed the effect he made."

"I don't know why he torments Desmond so. I suppose he recognises that there's no real feeling there."

It was dark as they stepped outside. The car showed white against the grey prison-like walls.

"Anyway," said Nancy, "he's certainly got some spirit!"

The next evening they went down to Penhallow, stopping at the farm on the top road to collect the key.

"I'd like you to come as well, Mr Laity," said Nancy, so the round-faced farmer got into the car and rode down the lane with them. The trees were all in bud, the ash still black but the sycamores beginning to unfold crinkled, yellowish-brown leaves. The new shoots on top of the pines were like little crosses held up against the sky. A woodpecker flew down the valley, making its laughing call.

The farmer unlocked the back door, and they went inside. It smelled closed-up and musty. The geranium plants needed watering. It was strange to be standing in the kitchen when Mr and Mrs Treloar had gone away, and the house was empty. Fran stood and listened.

Nancy went straight through to the hall. "Damn!" Fran heard her say. She came back. "The book's not there," she said. "We'll have to search for it."

They looked in all the obvious places, behind the hall table, beside the bed, on the dresser, and, remembering Mrs Treloar, the less obvious ones like the oven and the meat safe. They began to go through cupboards and drawers.

Suddenly Fran caught a glimpse of a shadow crossing the window, and then someone opened the door. Desmond and Vera Rowe came through the curtain. They stood just inside the room and stared at Nancy and Fran, kneeling by the open bottom drawer of the dresser.

There was a look of triumph on their faces, as though they had caught them red-handed going through the old couple's possessions. And then the look of triumph turned to one of embarrassment, as they realised that they had been discovered with—as it seemed to them—the same intention.

Nancy was the first to speak. "Well, we have visitors," she said.

"What are you doing here?" asked Desmond gruffly.

She put the letter on the table, and called to Mr Laity. The farmer came in from the sitting-room, and the Rowes' expressions changed again as they saw him.

"We're looking for Mr Treloar's address book," she said. "Perhaps you have some idea where it is?"

Desmond turned on his heel and went, slamming the door behind him with a bang which shook the whole house.

"I don't know why he didn't ask us to fetch it," said Vera. "After all, we *are* relatives."

"Were you looking for anything in particular?" asked Nancy.

"No, we just thought we'd keep an eye on the place."

They continued the search and then Desmond came back from the car, bursting through the door and slamming the address book down on the table.

"Come on!" he muttered between clenched teeth, and his wife followed him out of the house.

"He wants to watch his blood pressure!" said Nancy. They packed up, and walked back up the track. The red car was jolting over the ruts at the top of the lane, and shot straight out on to the road.

"What do you think he was doing with the address book?" Fran asked, when they had dropped Mr Laity.

"I suppose he'd picked it up earlier, to see who's in it," said Nancy. "They've obviously gone through everything in the house."

"Do you think they'd take anything?"

"No, they just want to know what's there." Nancy laughed. "Poor Desmond, I feel quite sorry for him. He's eaten up with greed and jealousy. I don't know what he's worried about, he'll probably get most of it anyway. But if he goes on like this, he won't live long enough to enjoy it!"

Mr Treloar clasped the address book with both hands. "That's all I want," he said. "Now everything can be settled, and I shall be easy in my mind." He lay back on the pillows and closed his eyes, then half opened them and swept a glance around his visitors, Mr and Mrs Rowe on one side of the bed and Fran and her mother on the other.

"I'd just like you to write your full names and address for me," he said, passing the book towards Fran.

Desmond Rowe shot bolt upright, and marched out into the other ward.

"Go on, you don't want that!" said Nancy.

"Write both your names."

Fran had taken the book; she looked at her mother. Nancy shrugged.

So she wrote her mother's name and her own on the appropriate page. He took the book back, and scrutinised the writing.

"That's very good," he said, with great satisfaction.

When they were back in the car, Fran asked her mother what she thought of Mr Treloar asking for their names and address when he was making his will.

"I shouldn't pay much attention to it," Nancy said. "He's just playing a game with Desmond. He's got him on tenterhooks and he's making the most of it. Old people have a lot of fun making their wills. I've seen it happen time and time again, it's their last taste of power. Almost every week someone says to me 'I won't forget you, nurse!' with a significant little nod, and I've never been left a penny. I wouldn't want it anyway. I shouldn't think about it, if I were you."

★

The Treloars were no longer patients of Nancy's, and she saw no need to go on visiting them in hospital, especially when it only upset the relatives. Frances, too, had started her exam revision, and had little time to spare. Two weeks went by without a visit.

When one of the nurses had to see a patient in Goonlaze House—which occasionally happened—it was Rosemary who went. She reported going to say hullo to Mr Treloar, rather apprehensively after their last encounter, and he was very pleasant to her. In fact, he asked her to write her name and address in his book. "He's forgiven you all right!" said Nancy. He sent them a message through Rosemary; he would dearly love to see them again.

They could not find him at first; he had been moved from the annexe to the general ward. Nancy asked a student nurse, and she led them up another flight of stairs, talking all the way about her training and how geriatric nursing was part of the course.

He was halfway down a long ward, asleep in bed. Fran thought he looked just like all the other old men, as though the spirit of the place was taking effect. It shocked her to see him looking so wasted.

"Come on, Tom!" called the student. "You've got visitors!"

He struggled awake, and seemed lost for a moment.

"Isn't he sweet!" said the girl. "He's a darling!"

She put her arms round him and kissed him on the side of the face. Fran disliked her intensely.

He ignored the nurse, and the life came back to his expression as he saw Fran and Nancy.

"I've missed you so much," he said, as he struggled up in the bed. There were tears in his eyes.

"Why, what's the matter?" asked Nancy.

"I don't think we'll ever get out of this place," he said. "I don't think we'll ever get home."

"Why's that?"

He reached in his locker and fumbled through the contents for a letter. He passed it to Nancy, who took it out of its envelope and held it for Fran to read as well.

> *Dear Cousin Tom,*
>
> *Sorry to hear that you and your wife are in hospital. As regards your proposition, everything would have to be cut and dried and put on a proper basis. If you make over everything to me, house, contents, etc, I will come and look after you as long as is necessary.*
>
> *Yours sincerely,*
> *Winifred.*

Nancy passed the letter back. "So that's the famous Cousin Win," she said. "Are you going to do it?"

"Why should she have the farm?" he asked angrily.

"If you want to stay there and have someone to look after you, it's the only way."

"I could pay her a wage."

"She won't accept that."

He plucked at the bedclothes. "I need someone to advise me. What do you suggest?"

"When did you last see this Cousin Win?"

"After the war, over thirty years ago."

"So you've no idea what she's like now."

"She was always a very capable woman."

"Yes, she sounds it," said Nancy sharply. "But it may be the best thing for you. Look, I think it would be reasonable to suggest a trial period. Write to her and invite her to stay for a fortnight when you come out of hospital, with no commitment on either side. After all, she might decide that she doesn't fancy *you*!"

Mr Treloar brightened considerably. "That's a very good idea," he said. "You always know what to do, I feel much better already!"

*

The hospital had done all they could for them. Mrs Treloar could now get about with a walking frame, and Mr Treloar was physically much fitter than when he had left the farm. Other patients were waiting for their beds. If the old couple had been destitute, they could have stayed, but as they had means they were expected to provide for themselves. The hospital social worker arranged for them to go into a private nursing home until the date had been agreed for the arrival of Cousin Win. Nancy heard of this through the surgery, and felt that she should go to see how they had settled in. Fran went with her.

It was a long drive to the sea-side town on the south coast where 'The Laurels' was situated, and they had difficulty finding the road, high up above the bay. It was an avenue of late Victorian or Edwardian villas, most of them now converted into holiday flats or lodging houses with names like 'Hotel Miramar'. The nursing home was right at the end of the cul-de-sac; it looked rather shabbier than the other houses, with peeling paintwork and a few tired-looking bushes—the laurels—in the front.

They followed the drive around to the back, and parked by the dustbins. This side of the house was covered with scaffolding, and there were piles of builder's rubble. The yellow brick walls all round were smeared with green mould. There was a general air of decay.

Fran could see Nancy's mouth getting tighter as she pursed her lips. They rang a door-bell, but no one came. They went through a conservatory, which would have been quite a pleasant place to sit in the sun, only it was filled with planks and old furniture. Some of the panes were missing and the wall was a livid green where there was a leak in the roof.

Mr and Mrs Treloar were sitting side by side in their first-floor room. She was in a low arm-chair and was wearing a man's dressing gown. He was dressed in his

94

brown tweed suit and tie, and was sitting on a wooden kitchen chair, his hand resting on his wife's shoulder. They both looked up as the door opened, Lettie staring through rather bleary spectacles.

They were delighted to see Nancy and Fran, as they had not had any visitors. The Rowes had always been at the hospital, but now they kept away.

"How do you manage those stairs?" asked Nancy.

"We can't," said Mr Treloar. Apparently when they arrived they were carried up to their room, with a great deal of difficulty, and there they had remained for three days. As the dining-room was on the ground floor, their meals were brought to them on a tray. They could not get to the common room, so they had seen no one except a few of the staff.

"Didn't the hospital make it clear that you'd have to be on the ground floor if there aren't any lifts?" asked Nancy. She was very cross. "All they want is to get patients out, without any concern about where they go."

She knelt beside Mrs Treloar. "Why aren't you dressed, my love?" She felt her ankles, which were bare beneath her nightdress; she had a pair of slippers on her feet. "You're freezing cold."

There was a small electric fire in front of them, with a flex snaking away to the wall. Nancy rubbed the old lady's feet.

"And you've got a sore on your heel!" she exclaimed. "It's too bad!"

She put her feet up on a pillow, and covered her legs with an eiderdown.

Fran looked around the room. It was high and narrow, with a nondescript fawnish wallpaper. The floor was covered with brown linoleum. Two single beds of un-equal height were pushed against the walls at one end, next to an unmatching wardrobe and a chest of drawers. A basin had been fixed under the sash window. Outside

95

the window was scaffolding, and beyond that the yellow brick wall shoring up the hillside.

Mr Treloar followed her eyes. "Fine views over the bay," he said, obviously quoting the nursing home's brochure.

How could he stand it? she thought. How could he be shut up in here, and still make jokes?

It was like keeping them in a cage. Their food was brought in and their excrement taken out, and all they could do all day long was to sit and look at an empty wall. It was a colourless room with no pictures, magazines or books and no radio or television. They just sat and waited.

Nancy had made the old lady comfortable, and was polishing her glasses.

"How much have you paid in advance?" she asked.

The old man smiled. "I had a real set-to with the matron," he said, enjoying the memory of the fight. "She wanted me to pay a month's advance, but I said I'd only pay a week at a time. She didn't like it, but she gave in."

"I think it's time I had a word with her," said Nancy. She gave the glasses a last rub, and hooked them back over the old lady's ears.

When she had gone, Mrs Treloar seemed to lose the confidence she had gained from Nancy's presence. She began to cry.

"Come on, now, Lettie!" her husband shouted. "You've got to be brave!"

"I want to go home," she sobbed.

"We've got to stay here and get our strength up," he said firmly. "It won't be for long, and then we can go home."

She made an effort, wiped away her tears, and then relapsed, worse than ever. "I don't know what we've done to deserve this," she wailed.

He patted her arm with clumsy affection. "We'll pull through," he said. "It'll be all right."

When Nancy came back she was carrying a vase of anemones of vivid purples and reds, a newspaper and a pile of colour supplements. She cheered up Mrs Treloar, and promised that she would do all she could to get things moving. The whole atmosphere was different when she was there.

"I've made it quite clear to the matron that the Treloars aren't on their own, that they've got someone to fight for them," she said, as they drove out of 'The Laurels'. "If they don't get a fair deal she's got me to contend with. She blamed it all on the hospital, and I can see her point. They don't give her any details, she had no idea how immobile they were. She said she wouldn't have taken them if she'd known. However, from now on they're going to dress her every day, and keep a watch on her heel. But I'm not going to let them stay a day longer than I can help."

"It's a dump," said Fran.

"And do you know how much they have to pay?" asked Nancy.

When she heard, Fran found it incredible. They each paid more than the average weekly wage of a working man.

Nancy made several phone calls as soon as they got home. She discovered that Cousin Win, who lived somewhere in the Midlands, was on the phone, and she spoke to her. It was arranged that she would arrive at Penhallow the following Saturday week.

A few days later she went back to the nursing home, one afternoon when Fran was at school. She helped Mr Treloar draft a letter giving seven days' notice of his intention to leave, and took it with his cheque to the matron, who was not very pleased to lose them so quickly, but there was nothing she could do about it.

She called on the Rowes, in their bungalow at the edge

97

of the town, and asked them to prepare the farm for the arrival of Cousin Win. They had heard of the proposed arrangement. They probably thought that Nancy was in league with her, for they saw conspiracies in everything. All Desmond's repressed violence burst out.

"For that bloody gold-digger!" he yelled. "I wouldn't go near the place!"

So she got the home help to go in and clean the farmhouse, alerted Mr Laity, and arranged for an ambulance to pick up the old people. She fetched Mr Treloar's cousin from the station herself. Cousin Win was an elderly lady and seemed very confused after her journey. Nancy thought that perhaps she had taken too many travel sickness tablets. She went to rest for a while on her bed before the arrival of Mr and Mrs Treloar.

It was a perfect day for the home-coming. The sun was shining and the sky was a deeper blue than Fran could ever remember. There was a light breeze blowing down the valley to the sea.

In the overgrown garden, she picked a large bunch of ferns and columbines, which grew like weeds amongst the rank grass. She added some early foxgloves which were flowering on the terraces, and returned to the house, finding a jug in the scullery and putting the flowers on the kitchen table. The old people were superstitious about flowers, she knew. There were some that you could bring into the house, others that had to stay outside. She hoped those she had picked were all right.

The windows were wide open, and the house smelt fresh and clean. The sunlight poured in, shining on the new green of the ferns, the delicate mauves and yellows of the columbines, the deep pinks and purples of the foxgloves. A few motes of dust hung in the light. Upstairs she could hear the distant voices of her mother and Cousin Win.

She walked slowly up the lane. In the last few days the

leaves had all come out on the trees, and the farmhouse and buildings had disappeared behind the sycamores. The white blossom on the thorn bushes had given way to a startling green; everything was bright and new.

She waited at the gate. The opposite hillside had changed colour completely, covered now with a new growth of bracken, and the bare rocks were surrounded by a sea of green fronds. Swallows darted through the air, high above the sides of the valley.

It was not long before the creamy-coloured ambulance came swaying down the lane. They were the men who had taken the Treloars away, so the place was no surprise to them. They came to a stop behind Nancy's car, and started to carry Mrs Treloar down to the house on a stretcher.

Mr Treloar appeared at the door of the ambulance, and gave her a wave. He tried to get down the step.

"You ought to wait," called Fran, reaching out to steady him. She felt sure he would fall, but he was determined to enter his home again on his own two feet.

She took his walking frame and held his arm tight. He put his full weight on her, and then he was safely on the ground. With his head down, he moved forward a few paces on his frame until he was clear of the ambulance. He stood and looked around.

Fran watched him as he gazed across the valley. She could feel his joy at seeing Penhallow, and on such a beautiful day of early summer, when perhaps he had thought never to see it again.

Then he set out to walk down the lane. With his lips pressed together in determination, he pushed the frame out in front of him, steadied it, and moved forward a few inches at a time. The path was stony and uneven, and the pulpit rocked dangerously. Fran hovered nearby, trying to see that it was safe. The rubber-studded feet crushed the garlic plants, and the smell from the bruised leaves and stems filled the air.

"Can you smell the garlic?" she asked.

He paused, and sniffed. Then he recognised it, and drew in several deep breaths.

The ambulance men were coming up the path, heads bowed beneath the trees, their blue uniforms dappled with the light filtering through the leaves. They offered to help, but the old man refused. They followed him down, supporting him on each side of the steep slope into the yard.

It was easier on the level. He lifted the frame forward, took a step with his left leg, and dragged his right leg up to it; each gain brought him closer to the open door. He was hunched over the pulpit. His silky white hair lifted in the light breeze, and the sun shone through it, as through the leaves.

Cousin Win rushed out of the door and tried to take his arm. He brushed her aside, and crossed the threshold. He made for his chair in the corner by the stove, and sat down, tired but triumphant.

His cousin put her arms around him and kissed him and tut-tutted about him walking down the lane on his own.

"I walked as I belong to do," he said shortly.

He did not seem to like all the attention. He looked round the room, as though trying to avoid her fussing. He admired the flowers—he called the columbines 'grannies' bonnets'—and thought everything looked very nice. Mrs Treloar sat opposite him, on her side of the fire.

"Well, Lettie," he said. "We've managed it. I told you we would. We've come home!"

Cousin Win was bustling about, getting everything organised, but not really achieving very much. It was time to leave them to it.

Fran and Nancy followed the ambulance men up the lane.

"Well, I can't see it lasting very long," said Nancy. "He doesn't like to be fussed. He'll put up with it for so long, but there'll be a row before the two weeks are up."

They drove home, stopping first in the village to do the weekend shopping. As they pulled up outside the garage they could hear the phone ringing inside the house.

"Blast!" said Nancy. "Who can that be?" It was supposed to be her weekend off duty.

She leaped out of the car and hurried into the house, followed by Fran. When her mother picked up the phone, Fran could hear the loud and deliberate voice of Mr Treloar, though she could not make out what he was saying.

"Oh no!" exclaimed Nancy.

The deep voice rumbled on.

"Oh well, I'll come over!" her mother said, without much grace. She replaced the phone and looked at Fran. "Back we go again!"

"Why, what's happened?"

"Mrs Treloar has had some sort of accident. I couldn't make it out exactly." She expelled her breath crossly. "And she's only been in the house two minutes!"

It was not more than an hour after leaving the farm, that they were once again plunging down the leafy lane. They hurried through the back door.

"Where is everyone?" called Nancy. The kitchen was empty, the house seemed deserted.

"Here!" called Cousin Win, coming out of the back scullery. Mr Treloar was there, too, standing in front of the lavatory door.

"What's the matter, Lettie?" he was calling.

"I'm quite all right," came a tiny voice beyond the door.

"What's going on?" asked Nancy, moving forward. She tried to ease the door open, but it held against something solid. She knelt down, and spoke at the base. "Are you on the floor, Lettie?"

"I'm quite all right," said Mrs Treloar.

Nancy could see nothing through the gap beneath the door. "We'll try the window," she said.

She and Fran went through the garden to the lavatory window. It was a small sash of frosted glass, open an inch or two at the top. Fran reached up and pulled it down as far as it would go. Then she put a knee on the window ledge and was able to pull herself up to look through.

At first it seemed very dark inside, after the bright sunshine, and her own figure filled the window space. But she quickly saw that the old lady had fallen forward from the toilet seat. She was lying with her head right against the door.

"Can you get through?" called Nancy.

Fran wriggled through the narrow space until she could get one leg in. Then she was able to draw the other leg through, step on to the lavatory seat and down on to the floor by the old lady's side.

She dragged her away from the door.

"I'm quite all right," she said.

But Fran was shocked when she saw her face. It was bleeding profusely from several cuts and abrasions, and one eye was closed. It looked raw and ugly.

Cousin Win opened the door, took one glance, and tried to get Mr Treloar back into the kitchen. He refused to budge. Then Nancy came round from the other side, and they lifted Mrs Treloar on to her bed, still saying that she was quite all right. Nancy rang for an ambulance, deciding that the cuts were far too bad to be treated at home; then she set about cleaning up her face.

They were the same ambulance men as before, joking about taking up residence at the farm. They carried her on the stretcher, Nancy going with her to the ambulance and reassuring her. For the second time they took her away from her home.

Fran and her mother drank a cup of tea in the farm-house kitchen before leaving. They were all thinking of Lettie.

"Whatever was she doing in the toilet?" asked Nancy.

"As soon as you left, she said she wanted to spend a penny," said Cousin Win. "So I took her to the toilet and left her. She seemed to be rather a long time, so I called to her, 'Are you all right, Lettie?' 'Yes, I'm quite all right,' she said. Then I tried the door. It wasn't locked, but I couldn't push it open. She had fallen against it."

"But I told you, she has a catheter. There was no need for her to go to the toilet."

"I didn't realise," said Cousin Win huffily. "I'm sorry, I'm sure."

"Dammee!" shouted Mr Treloar, slapping his leg, as it dawned on him that the accident need not have happened at all. "Of course she didn't!"

He blamed himself. He looked worried about his wife, and disappointed after all his hopes for their return to Penhallow. Fran could not bear to see him so dispirited. She went out into the garden, and wandered down through the wood.

It was so cruel, she thought. All that they had longed for had been destroyed. They had thought that every-thing would be all right; they would be in their own home, with someone to look after them. And within two hours Lettie had been taken away again, in circumstances which were like a heartless practical joke.

She reached the stream. She had pulled off a stalk of bracken on the way, and she stood on the bridge, shred-ding the fronds and scattering the pieces into the running water.

★

Mrs Treloar was admitted to the general hospital. She had stitches in her face, and was kept in for two nights, then transferred to Goonlaze House. She now needed full-time care, and it seemed unlikely that she would ever return to the farm, though Mr Treloar never gave up hope of having her back.

He was now a patient of Nancy's again, and either she or Rosemary visited him daily. He became more and more impatient with Cousin Win. He was working harder than ever to look after her, instead of her looking after him, and she annoyed him in many ways. She was not very happy with the arrangement either, and she told Nancy that she did not think it was proper for her to be alone in the house with the old man.

It all came to a head before the end of the week. Moving about on his walking frame, he had made two enormous pasties, which he served for dinner. Cousin Win toyed with hers, cutting off the pastry crust and eating only a little of the meat and vegetables inside.

He told her he could not stand pernickety women, and she could either eat her pasty or go. She said she would not be shouted at or dictated to. She packed her bags, rang for a taxi, and left.

"So that's the end of Cousin Win," said Nancy, when he told her the next day.

"A good job too!" he said. The battle had raised his spirits higher than they had been for a few days, since Lettie had gone.

"You might regret it," said Nancy. "You might have to plead with her to come back one day."

"Never!" said the old man, with great determination. "I'll never have her in this house again!" He was going to stay on and look after himself. Without having to care for his wife, he could just about manage.

Lettie could not remain in Goonlaze House, and Nancy began looking for a nursing home not too far away, so that Mr Treloar could visit her. The best home was run by her old friend the matron, but she had no vacancies. The others all had to be of a certain standard in order to be licensed, but there was something about each of them that made her hesitate. One was too formal, another too informal; in one there were too many extras added to the bill, in another the food was good but the nursing non-existent.

And then by a stroke of luck (it was Nancy's phrase) an old lady died in Stennack hospital, and her bed became vacant. Although it was no more than a village, Stennack had had a large mining population in the nineteenth century, with a Miners' Hospital built by public subscription after a disaster in which many men had been killed or injured. The hospital had been taken over by the Health Service, and turned into an old people's home. There were about forty beds, three-quarters of them occupied by women.

Lettie Treloar was moved once more, by now in considerable confusion as to where she was.

Frances was in the height of the examination season, and the weather continued sunny and warm. Day after day, sitting at a desk in a long row she poured out all that she had absorbed in the last five years about maths and French, history and geography, English literature and biology. On the days between the exams, she stayed at home and revised for the next.

"It'll be marvellous when it's over!" she said.

"When what's over?" asked Nancy, who was filling in her time sheet.

"The exams, of course!"

"You'll have others," said Nancy cheerfully. "My nursing exams seemed to go on for years."

"Thanks!" said Fran. "I suppose one day I shall finish with them."

She sent a message to Mr Treloar that she would start visiting him again once she had taken her last exam. She heard about him from her mother. Nancy was trying to make arrangements for him to visit his wife in the old people's home. She could usually find some active retired person to provide transport, or the Rotary Club would provide drivers, but in this case there was the problem of getting Mr Treloar up the path, as well as finding someone willing to take his car down the lane.

Mr Laity took him to the home first of all, with Nancy helping. Mr Treloar made his way slowly on his walking frame up to the bottom of the lane. It was a great achievement, but the visit was not such a success. Most of the time Lettie did not remember that she had a husband and that her home was at the farm. She remembered above all the farm where she grew up, and sometimes she thought that she was in South Africa. But when Tom was there at the side of her bed, the recent past came back to her and she cried to go home.

The Rowes had turned up again, both at the hospital and at the farm. At the weekend Nancy said that Desmond was scything the long grass in the garden, and that he seemed to be doing it quite cheerfully. He was quite friendly towards her; he probably thought that she had helped to drive away Cousin Win.

Three

The exams were over, and one of the first things Fran
wanted to do in the weeks of freedom that followed was
to visit the seal cave described by Mr Treloar. There was
a boy at school called David who was interested in caving
and rock-climbing; she had met him when the sixth-
formers had shared the fifth-year common room. She had
told him about the cave, and he wanted to go as well.

He picked her up at the house. He rode a bright orange
and yellow Japanese motor-bike, a Suzuki. She had heard
him talking to other boys about his Suzy, and for a while
had thought it was his girl friend.

He had a bright orange helmet on his head and a rope
coiled over one shoulder and around his body. On the
rack behind the pillion seat was a rucksack with a white
crash helmet strapped on top. He took it off for Fran to
wear.

She tucked her hair inside the helmet; she felt as if she
was in a strange, cut-off world. Her head was top-heavy,
and she could not see clearly through the visor. It was
steaming over with her breath, and she pushed it up.
Dave fixed the strap beneath her chin, and she went to sit
on the passenger seat.

He was saying something to her, but she could not
hear.

"What?" she shouted.

"Wait a minute, I'll just kick her over!"

She imagined him taking a kick at the bike and knocking it off its stand, but he stood astride it and kicked down the starter. It burst into life.

He pushed forward and the stand went up with a bang. She mounted behind him, finding the rests for her feet. He turned his head.

"Lean the way I do!" he shouted.

He moved off with a quick swerve to left and to right to get on to the correct side of the road, taking her by surprise. She held on tight.

The village passed in a blur, and then he accelerated away from it. The air blew around her, her trouser legs flapped; she felt cold and exposed, even though she was sheltered by his back.

Then he took a track which led to the cove, and as the road was not made up, he had to go slowly. They bumped and jolted along, Fran rising and falling on the pillion. As they came over the top, she could look down into the valley, but because of the curve, Penhallow was out of sight. They dropped down around hairpin bends to the beach, and he stopped by the ruined walls of an engine house.

They had worked out the times of the tide, and planned to have an hour each side of low water. Fran had told Nancy where she was going, in case they were stranded. She thought her mother might make some objections, but she probably knew that they would not take any risks. As local people it would be too embarrassing to have to be rescued like the holiday-makers who knew nothing of the cliffs and the sea, and often got into difficulty.

She was glad to take off her helmet and shake her hair free. Dave put the rucksack on his back, and they set off across the beach, sinking at first into grey sand and then climbing over rocks. The tide was well out, the sea a bluish-green, with patches of cloud shadow. The surface looked hillocky, with little peaks crested with white.

They had risen to a sort of platform of rock below the headland. There were many initials carved on the shelves and steps, and the oldest date she could find was in the eighteen-eighties. There was a whole collection of war-time names and dates.

Dave gave them a glance, and started climbing down to the gravel beach below the height. Fran searched until she found what she was looking for. On the rock face were two bold capital letters and a date: T.T. 1906. They were chiselled deep into the stone, in a style which some-how looked of its period, though she could not have explained why. They were made to last, unlike those which were merely scratched on the surface. She was delighted to find them there. She would never have wanted to cut her own name in stone, and yet she admired young Tom Treloar's confident assertion of him-self and his continuity.

"Hey!" Dave was calling her from the beach below, and she climbed down to him. Beyond them was a stretch of massive boulders, fallen in times past from the cliff face, and they clambered over them, leaping from rock to rock. The waves surged forward, rushing be-tween the rocks and splashing over the top. The force of the water made Fran feel dizzy if she looked at it.

They leaped down on to a small beach. The tide had just cleared it, and there was not a mark on the smooth stretch of sand. They ran across it, and turned to look back at their two sets of footprints. No holiday-makers ever found their way here.

Before them stood the arched mouth of the cave, as big as a chapel. The tide had built up the sand across the entrance, trapping a large pool; the sunlight reflected from the surface struck the roof of the cave, so that a shimmering light played over the stone.

They waded through. As they broke the surface, the light on the roof shattered; it danced frantically until they reached the sand beyond, and then gradually it settled down. A few drips of water fell from above, and the chill of the cavern struck them.

The rocks rising out of the sandy floor, with smaller pools around them, were covered with a shiny black seaweed. Mr Treloar said that this was laver; they used to boil it and eat it as a vegetable. She scraped a sample into a plastic bag.

Some of the rocks of the cave wall were a dark red, the colour of dried blood, others a vivid green amongst the browns and greys. At the back of the cave she turned. The sea and sky were framed by the great arch, and everything beyond it was bright and dazzling. She thought of the seals coming in on the waves; there was no sign of any today. She tried to absorb it all, to notice every detail so that she could tell Mr Treloar. He would be able to see it through her eyes.

The tunnel was still lit from the entrance, and some way ahead Dave was standing in a patch of light brought by a shaft at an angle from the cliff face. Beyond, everything was black. He produced a torch from his haversack, and they set off in its light through what was now a man-made tunnel. It was just high enough to stand upright though not to walk two abreast, and the walls were squared. It rose slightly all the way; it must have been made to drain the workings. From time to time there were openings overhead. They shone the torch into the holes where the tin-ore had been taken out, some of them great, empty caverns. One had iron stakes driven into the side, which the miners had climbed up and stood on to work.

It was by now very cold, in a damp, clammy way. They looked for specimens of stone. Fran found an attractive quartz, but there was nothing much left with any tin in it. Hopefully, they picked up a few pieces.

They came to a vertical shaft in the roof above. It had

metal rungs set into the side, eaten with rust. There was no light at the top, so it was probably boarded over. It must have been the shaft that Mr Treloar had descended on his way to the cave when the tide was in.

She thought of him bringing the things he found on the beach up through the tunnel and storing them here, before raising them through the shaft. She thought of him climbing up and down the metal rungs. Although the workings were abandoned, and no one had been there for years, his presence seemed to pervade the place.

They walked back to the cave. The light was dazzling; she could see nothing at first, only soak in the warmth of the sun. Then she saw, out at sea, what she thought for a moment was a dog's head.

"Look, it's a seal!" she shouted excitedly, and was immediately afraid that she had frightened it away.

But it was not in the least disturbed. It floated in the water, its head sticking up and turning from side to side. It watched them with curiosity. She could see its whiskers.

Then it put its head down and its body pushed across the surface before it sank out of sight.

The next day Nancy intended to visit Mr Treloar immediately after surgery, picking up Fran on the way. Fran had been waiting over an hour when the car drew up outside and the horn blew twice. She slammed the door and joined her mother.

"The surgery was packed with holiday-makers," said Nancy, to explain why she was so late. "Most of them had sunburn, two had caught their fingers in deck-chairs, and one had smashed his thumb with a mallet putting up a wind-break. I attended to them all, and it occurred to me whilst I was doing it, the doctor gets a visitor's fee for each of them. He made a tidy sum this morning, and he didn't even see them. I did all the work, and for no extra pay. I shall have to rush around like mad for the rest of the day in order to catch up. There's something wrong there somewhere."

Fran was impatient to show the old man the pieces of rock, and as soon as they arrived she took them out of her bag and placed them on the table, while he watched with keen interest. Nancy disappeared into the scullery, and Fran handed the stones one by one to Mr Treloar. He studied them very carefully, weighing them in his hand.

"I reckon there's some tin in that one," he was saying, when he saw Nancy coming into the kitchen with a bowl of hot water. He stopped, and watched her suspiciously as she put it on the table. Then she put on her apron.

"What are you doing that for?" he asked.

"I'm going to do your feet, Mr Treloar."

"I don't want my feet done," he said. He turned back to Fran. "These stones are very interesting."

"And I want to do them," said Nancy. "So who do you think's going to win?"

"Ah well," he said, handing the stones back to Fran. "You will, I suppose. But I'm not going to have them done in here."

He heaved himself up on his frame, and Nancy followed him into the bedroom across the hall. Fran could hear splashing and laughter, as no doubt the bottoms of his feet were tickled.

"Right, that's all!" said the old man.

"I'll just do your top half while I'm about it," said Nancy. "It's time you had a clean shirt. Come on, let's have your vest off as well!"

There were more sounds of complaint, although obviously he was going to give in. Fran remembered how she used to moan when Nancy bathed her as a small child. When she dried her with the towel, she rubbed so vigorously she almost took the skin off. She felt a fellow sympathy with Mr Treloar.

Then there were sounds of real complaint, unlike the good-humoured ones before. He almost bellowed. "I will *not* take my trousers off," he shouted. "I've done that part myself!"

"All right," said Nancy. "I'll take your word for it."

A little later, surprisingly quickly, they were coming back into the kitchen, the old man looking pink-complexioned and fresh, like a baby, his hair sticking out around his head.

"Does she treat you like that?" he asked humorously.

"She used to," said Fran. "I know what it feels like."

"She had the shirt off my back before I knew it."

He sat back in his chair and looked around with the air he always had when he was about to come out with something particularly good.

"Your mother," he said very deliberately, "is the fastest stripper in the business!"

They all laughed, and Fran wondered if he was conscious of the two ways in which it could be taken. Then she caught sight of the mischievous look in his eye, and decided that he knew exactly what he was saying.

When Nancy had gone, he identified what by now looked like a plastic bag of black mud as laver, and said that he would fry it up for his breakfast. It was lovely with a bit of liver and bacon.

She told him about her visit to the seal cave, and he questioned her closely about the amount of sand on the floor, the size of the pools, the condition of the timber in the mine, so that he knew it almost as well as if he had climbed through the tunnels himself. He remembered every bit as it was, noted every change, and recalled the day he had carved his initials. Finally she told him that she had seen a seal.

"Do you know," he said, "when I was a boy I used to play a mouth organ. I used to take it down to the cave and play. And there was one old seal who would always pop his head out of the water to listen. He used to love music, but particularly if it was a bit slow and mournful. I reckon that's where all the stories of mermaids come from."

Fran pictured the farm lad at the turn of the century, standing on the wild sea shore playing mouth-organ music to the seals. The thought of it thrilled her, like music itself.

Mrs Treloar was poorly. On her rounds Nancy had been to see her at the old people's home, and thought that she was going downhill fast. "She's got a roaring urinary infection," she said. "She had no idea who I was. I said I'd go and see her husband, and she said, 'Didn't you know, dear? I lost him years ago!'"

She had gone to the farm to prepare Mr Treloar, without alarming him. She warned him that he might be called out at any time. He had accepted now that she would never come home, while he would carry on as long as he could on his own at the farm. It might be hard in the winter, but that was a long way ahead.

There was one thing which worried him. "Do you think my mind will go like Lettie's?" he asked Nancy. It was what he feared most.

"I'm sure it won't," she said. "You're not the sort."

"How do you think I'll go?"

She did not try to laugh it off. "You'll probably have a heart attack," she said.

"I don't think I shall last long after Lettie's gone."

He shed a few tears for her, and then he asked, "Do you think she could sign a cheque?"

"Mr Treloar!" exclaimed Nancy. "You old rogue! She can't even hold a teaspoon, leave alone a pen!"

But he was only trying to be practical. She had always paid household bills out of her account, and now it would have to come out of his. Nancy promised to get help to sort out financial matters.

"I'm not at all sure about Mrs Treloar," said Nancy to Fran. "You never know. She's just running down slowly, and it could take a long time."

"Do you think I should go to see him tomorrow?"

"Oh yes," said Nancy. "He's looking forward to it."

He had a board on the table when she went into the kitchen. It was a many-sided piece of mahogany, marked out in a grid with lines of white paint, and he was waiting for her to ask what it was.

"What's this?" she asked, picking it up. It had a pattern of holes for wooden pegs, set out in four courts around a central court.

"I was reminded of it when you went to the seal cave the other day," he said.

"It looks like a game," said Fran.

"One day I was walking through those tunnels and I got into a part of the mine I'd never been in before. I had an acetylene lamp with me, and in the light I saw something stuffed into a gap above a beam. I took it out, and it was a piece of oilskin. I unrolled it, and inside were twenty-five little wooden figures. They were beautifully carved. Twenty-four of them were geese and one was a fox. I wrapped them up again and put them on the beam, thinking I'd pick them up on my way back. That day I walked on and on. The tunnels connect with other mines, and there are miles and miles of them. But when I came to go back, I couldn't find the way. I thought I was lost, I thought I'd stay down there for ever. It was the only time in my life that I was really afraid. Then I saw a tunnel I recognised, and I hurried back to the part I knew, leaving the wooden figures behind. I went back again to try and fetch them, many times, but I could never find the spot."

"So they are still there," said Fran.

"Yes, they're still down there, somewhere." He looked as though he regretted not being able to set off into the tunnels again, on one more search for the missing pieces.

"But what were they?"

"I told old Billy Moyle, and he said it was a game of Fox and Geese. The old miners used to play it underground when they had their croust. He drew out the board for me, and I made up this one, from a piece of mahogany off the beach. I always meant to carve the figures, but I never got round to it . . . Shall we have a game?"

There was a glint in his eyes, the look he always had when he was about to do battle.

"You'll have to show me," said Fran.

"I'll be the fox," he said, with a sense of the rightness of it. He took a box of matches out of his pocket, and breaking off the heads placed six in the holes of each of the four outside pens. Then he placed the fox in the centre, an upright match with its head still intact.

"You have to try to pen me in, so that I can't move," he said. "I shall try to take you."

"How will you do that?"

"I'll jump over you, like draughts."

They made a few moves. Before long Fran saw that two of her pieces were at risk and that wherever she moved she could only protect one of them. She moved a piece forward to fill one of the spaces.

Mr Treloar glanced up at her, his face showing no emotion. He reached forward and very slowly and deliberately, with his thick, slightly trembling fingertips, he moved the peg and took her goose.

A little later the same thing happened, and then after that the fox rampaged through the geese, taking piece after piece almost at will, until the final piece fell.

He sat back, exuding satisfaction. He had enjoyed that.

"The fox is bound to win," said Fran.

They set up the board again, and this time Fran was the fox. Gradually he brought the geese forward in a double row until the fox was pushed out of the centre. Then she could only move to and fro within the pen until every space around her was filled solid with geese.

"The geese are bound to win," said Fran, revising her opinion.

"They are if they don't make a mistake," said Mr Treloar. "But if they make one mistake, the fox must be ready to take advantage of it. They can still win with one piece down, they can win with two pieces down though it's difficult. But if they've lost three pieces, then they haven't a chance."

Fran thought she had learned something about the game. "Let me be the geese again," she said.

She was really annoyed when she gave a piece away, and the old man took it triumphantly. But she did not make another slip, and although it took her a long time, she eventually cornered him.

He was pleased that she had won, but she realised that now she had got the idea of the game, it did not matter greatly to her whether she won or lost. It mattered a lot to Mr Treloar; he loved to win, and when she played the fox she never beat him.

She went back to school briefly before the end of term to begin the sixth-form courses. Many of the students did not know whether they would be coming back into the sixth form or not, and no one took the work very seriously. There were a lot of free periods, spent in the common room or in the coffee bar, or sitting outside in the sun.

She was almost dozing, her legs stretched out to get a tan, a book on her lap. Behind her the floor-to-ceiling windows of the common room caught the sun; on one side was the great bulk of the sports hall. She could smell the newly-mown grass, and could hear the tractor which pulled the cutters. Through half-closed eyes she could see the playing fields stretching away to a row of semi-detached houses in the distance.

She wondered what Mr Treloar would make of it, knowing only the village school with its stone walls and high windows, its four classrooms, its boys' yard and girls' yard.

David came and sat down next to her. She described the set of Fox and Geese, wrapped in oilcloth, which was still sitting undisturbed on a beam, far below the ground.

A girl who was lying in the grass not far away lifted her head. She had unbuttoned her blouse and pulled it down off her shoulders, which had turned red in the sun. It was Shirley Rowe.

"What are you planning to take from the old man?" she said.

"Nothing," said Fran coolly.

"I don't believe it," said Shirley. "You're after all you can get."

"That's not true. I haven't taken anything from him."

"Oh no?" Shirley said sarcastically. "What about the brass from the ship?"

"He made me take it."

"I bet he had a hard job to persuade you! Same as the five pound note, I expect!"

Fran felt alarmed. How did Shirley Rowe know about the five pound note?

"I bought him some tapes," she said.

"Tapes!" exclaimed Shirley. "What does an old man want tapes for?"

"He's recording his memories." She felt that she was too much on the defensive; she had no need to explain everything when she was completely in the right. Yet Shirley could make her seem to be in the wrong. She had been taken by surprise; she had been lying in the sun and suddenly this argument had burst into life, like a grass fire.

"And what happened to the frying pan?"

"The frying pan?" she echoed. This was too ridiculous. "I've no idea!"

"You know, the copper one with a date on it, hanging in the fireplace."

"Oh, you mean the warming pan."

"All right, the warming pan, then. You're so high and mighty about it, but you're not above taking it."

"I know nothing about it," said Fran.

"Well, my dad says it's gone and it's worth a lot of money. And he thinks that you've got it. Else why would you go down there so often? You're not a member of the family, it's nothing to do with you."

"I can choose my own friends."

"Friend!" scoffed Shirley. "He's old enough to be your great-grandfather! He's old and decrepit, he's smelly, he's disgusting . . ."

"I think he's very interesting," said Fran.

"You're a bloody gold-digger," said Shirley. She sounded just like her father.

Dave had been listening to them. "Girls! Girls!" he appealed, raising his hands and making a joke of it.

Shirley lay down in the grass again, with just the blonde top of her head showing and a glimpse of two raw shoulders. The quarrel smouldered on, breaking into flame from time to time.

"Anyway, my dad will be around to your house to fetch it back," said Shirley, lifting her head.

"He won't find it."

"I suppose you've sold it."

"I've never touched it."

Her conscience was quite clear, and yet she was troubled. Whatever happened it would involve Nancy, and it was the last thing that Nancy wanted, to be caught up in family disputes. It might be best if she stopped

119

seeing the old man. But he looked forward to her visits, and why should he suffer for the sake of family quiet? She was not going to stop going there, just to satisfy the mean-minded Rowes.

But she felt a sinking feeling inside. Unlike Mr Treloar, she had no relish for a fight.

When Nancy came in, she had been to see Lettie. Mr Treloar's neighbour had agreed to take him regularly to the hospital, once a week, and they had both been there.

"She looked dreadful," said Nancy. "Tom looked at me and he said, 'She's dying, isn't she?' The pupils of her eyes were pinpointed, I could see she was full of drugs. 'Do you know Tom's here?' I said. 'Where is he?' she said, and she was looking straight at him. 'Mrs Treloar, are you eating sweets?' I asked her. 'She's been asking for sweets,' said Mr Treloar, 'so I've been giving her some.' 'You ought to have more sense, Tom,' I said. 'You know she doesn't know what she's saying. You'll choke her.' Her mouth was stuffed full of wine gums. I put my finger in and hooked them all out. 'What are you doing to me?' she complained.

"I had a word with the sister. She said they'd had a terrible night with her, she was shouting and swearing and upsetting everyone else. She said she would never have thought an old lady would have known some of the language she came out with. They had to give her drugs in the end.

"It's a complete change of character. It's very sad, when she was always so gentle. They'll have to keep her heavily sedated from now on.

"So I told Mr Treloar that Lettie wasn't dying just yet, that she was sleepy because of the drugs they were giving her, and that she would probably be like that whenever he saw her. But I can't see her lasting very long."

Fran had to tell her mother about the quarrel. If the

Rowes were going to make accusations against her, it would be best for her to know beforehand. She told her what Shirley Rowe had said.

Nancy was not very pleased about the five pound note. "Did you give him back the change?"

"No," said Fran. "He wouldn't take it."

"You could have left it on the table."

"I know, but . . ." She sighed with exasperation. "All this fuss about money!" The poor old lady was dying, and all people seemed to bother about were trivial things, like who had her warming pan.

"Well, people *do* fuss about money, especially if they're relatives."

"How did the Rowes know, anyway?"

"It always comes out. They're obviously watching everything very closely. I had no idea the warming pan had gone. Well, if Desmond comes round here making accusations, I shall give him something to think about. But I don't think he will, he's too much of a coward. He just mutters behind your back. It's not very pleasant if they say things about you, but you must do what you think is right."

Nancy was gradually getting to know the staff at the hospital. Sister Thomas and Sister Williams had diametrically opposed attitudes to nursing the elderly, and as soon as one went off duty the other instituted a different régime. When Sister Williams came on for the night and discovered the amount of drugs that Mrs Treloar was being given, she cut the dose down by half.

For a while the old lady was quiet, and then just as everyone was settling down for the night, she started. She screamed and shouted, she tore all her bedclothes off, she threw her beaker across the ward. It took three nurses to get her medicine into her. She refused to take it at first, closing her mouth and opening it only to bite one of the nurses. "They're trying to murder me!" she screamed. "Three to one, it's not fair!"

When Nancy called in the morning she was still wide awake. Something came flying across the ward at her and instinctively she grabbed and caught it. There was a bottom set of false teeth in her hands.

"They aren't mine!" cried Mrs Treloar, who had taken them out and thrown them. "I don't want them!"

Another old lady in the same ward could not bear it any longer. "Please take me away from here!" she was crying.

"She's just not Lettie any more," said Nancy to Fran.

Frances reached the end of her term, and as soon as the holidays began, she started work as she had done for the last two summers at a local guesthouse. She worked a split day, serving breakfast in the morning and washing up afterwards, cleaning and tidying, having a long, free afternoon, and returning in the evening to help with the dinner.

On her first free afternoon she went to see Mr Treloar. She rode her bicycle to the farm, cycling through lanes which seemed narrow with summer growth in the verges. White clusters of cow parsley grew as high as her shoulder, and there was a reddish haze of sorrel amongst the heads of grasses along the stone banks.

She took her tape-recorder, and intended to spend the time recording. She wanted him to tell the story of how he found and lost the carved wooden pieces of the Fox and Geese, but his heart was not in it.

"Lettie's very poorly," he said after a while.

This was what Nancy had told him, without going into the distressing details of how she had changed.

"There's something I should like you to do for me," he went on. "I should like to go through all Lettie's things and sort them out properly. She's always been one for keeping letters and postcards, all sorts of odds and ends. There are drawers and boxes full of stuff, and I don't think she'll ever be able to do it herself. I should like you to help me get it all straight."

Fran hesitated; she was on the edge of getting involved in family affairs again. She would rather carry on tape-recording.

"It's a family matter," she said. "Why don't you ask Shirley?"

"Huh!" snorted Mr Treloar, as though she had said something stupid for the first time since he had known her. "I want to sort it all out before *they* get hold of it. I'd like you to carry a drawer out here, and put it on the table. Then we could look it through, and burn everything we don't want to keep."

"All right," she agreed.

She brought a drawer from the chest of drawers in the bedroom. Lettie had hoarded everything, and there were bills and receipts, letters and postcards, old photographs and newspaper cuttings, some going back to the beginning of the century. There were stamps with the heads of Edward VII and George V on the letters, and receipts with old-fashioned writing in black ink. There was a Gold Flake tin, with other cigarette and tobacco tins and several small caskets.

Fran thought it looked fascinating, and she knew that she would enjoy going through the contents. But she felt, too, that she was invading someone else's privacy. It represented the whole life of the old lady, all her secrets and treasured personal possessions. It was not for a stranger to investigate, while she was lying ill and dying, only a shell of her former self.

She started to pass some papers to Mr Treloar.

"We'll look them through," he said, "and then put them out for burning."

It distressed her to think of burning any of it. Even a

receipt which had lain around for fifty years had staked some sort of claim to existence. "You ought to keep it all," she said.

"No, we've got to sort it out," he said, with the same determination.

She made separate piles on the table, one for jewellery and knick-knacks, one for photographs, one for postcards. There were postcards embroidered with silk flags, sent from France during the First World War. "You can't destroy these," she said. "You've got to keep all the postcards."

She picked up a postcard-sized photograph. It was a posed studio portrait, faded brown with the years; the oval image was misty at the edges, but the girl stared boldly at the camera with her dark, lively eyes.

"Who's that?" she asked.

"That's Lettie, of course," he said.

As soon as she was told she could see the resemblance; she could trace the old lady's features in this girl's face. She knew that Lettie had not always had hollow eyes and drawn cheeks, with folds of skin around her neck, and yet she had never thought that she could really be as young as this. It made her youth seem real, and her age poignant.

"She was very beautiful," she said.

She passed the photograph to Mr Treloar, who stared silently at it. What thoughts went through his mind? she wondered. How could he bear to look at it for so long?

"How did you meet her?" she asked.

"I've always known Lettie," he said. "She went to the village school with me. Then her family emigrated to South Africa, and I didn't see her for many years, but I never forgot her. When my father died and I took over the farm, I thought it was time I got married. I looked around, but there were only Pascoe's three sisters, and I didn't fancy any of them. I could only think of this maid who had gone off to South Africa. After a lot of thought, I wrote her a letter. I wondered if she would like a holiday in the old country, and I invited her to stay at the farm, to see how we got on together, with a view to marriage. She came, and stayed."

"Did she keep your letter?" asked Fran.

"I expect so, she kept everything," said Mr Treloar.

They searched through the drawer and found an envelope with a South African stamp. It was Lettie's reply to the original letter, a very formal acceptance of his invitation. At the end was a slightly more personal note; she wrote that she had very fond memories of the farm and looked forward to seeing it again.

Next they found a letter addressed to her, care of the shipping company's office in Suez. She had received the letter on board ship, on her way home. It was written from the farm, in the large, rounded script that Fran recognised as Tom's. It was dated in June, and said that very shortly now they would meet again. The weather had been very good, and he had most of the hay harvest in. He was working very hard to get it all finished before she arrived, so that he would have a few days to take her around Cornwall.

But they could not find the first letter.

"I should like to see it again," said Mr Treloar. "It cost me some trouble that letter, I can tell 'ee. I took more pains with that than I've ever done with anything else."

Fran asked if he had a photograph of himself at that time, and he told her where to find one in another drawer. It was immediately recognisable; he had the same long face and firm features. His hair was cut close to his head and he wore his suit as though it was unfamiliar. He stared at her out of the past, and Fran felt a little disappointed. He looked handsome, jaunty and aggressive. She did not think she would have liked him as much as she did now.

She looked through some of the boxes of jewellery. There were several Victorian brooches and rings, and then she picked up a string of amber beads. They glowed in the light from the kitchen window.

"Do you like them?" asked Mr Treloar, looking up from the letter he was reading.

"They're beautiful," said Fran.

"They were my mother's," he said. "I want you to have them, for all the work you've done."

She shook her head. "I won't take anything," she said.

She carried the sheets of paper and torn envelopes into the yard and dropped them into an empty dustbin. She set light to them, and lifted them with a stick from time to time so that the flames caught. She was standing back, watching the specks of paper ash rise into the clear sky, when her mother and Desmond Rowe came down the lane together. He looked at her suspiciously.

She followed them into the house.

"Oh!" said Nancy straight away. "Your copper warming pan has gone!"

The old man scowled, and pressed his lips together.

"I hope the knockers haven't found their way down here," she went on. "You haven't let an antique dealer have it, have you?"

"I can do what I like with my own possessions," said Mr Treloar, beginning to get angry. "I can give whatever I want to whoever I want, and nobody's going to stop me. I haven't been certified yet."

He was staring at Desmond, who could hardly take his eyes off the piles of paper, stamps, photos and jewellery on the table.

Desmond went off to cut back the sides of the lane; the bushes and trees had grown in again. As soon as he had gone, Mr Treloar told them that he had given the pan to a niece who had visited him and kept admiring it, saying how lovely it was and how she had always wanted a warming pan, until eventually he had told her to take it. "But I don't want Desmond to know," he said.

"Why not?" asked Nancy.

"Because it's none of his business," the old man said. And then he added, with a glint in his eye, "And I want to keep him guessing."

"You won't believe what I'm going to tell you," said Nancy. She had just come in, while Fran was about to go out for her evening shift. "I went to see Mrs Treloar today, and she was as bright as a button. She was her old self, very gracious. 'I'm *so* glad you've come,' she said. 'I *do* like to have visitors, and no one ever comes to see me.' Her mind was completely clear, and a few days ago she was throwing her teeth at me. She's amazing!"

Nancy arranged for Mr Treloar to go and see his wife twice a week, now that she had pulled through her illness. "She needs someone to talk to, someone who can keep her memory alive, not the other old ladies in the ward. I can't spare her more than a few minutes, but if I talk to her about Tom and the farm it all comes back to her. Get him to take some of those letters and photos you've been sorting through, it'll be a stimulus for her."

Fran continued cycling to the farm on two afternoons a week, to do some 'searching', as Mr Treloar called it. Gradually they were getting all the drawers into order, but it was a slow process as the old man kept finding things that he had forgotten. They came across a bundle of old photographs, and he stared for a long time at a portrait of his father, a full-bearded Victorian gentleman in a high-buttoned jacket.

"Did you ever know your father?" he asked her. And then as soon as he had said it he became very agitated. He had spoken without thinking.

"No," said Fran lightly.

"My dear, I'm sorry, I shouldn't have mentioned it."

"That's all right," she said. "I don't mind." He was so concerned that she might be hurt, so full of regret for saying the wrong thing. "It doesn't matter to me at all."

"I could bite my tongue off!" he said. "You'll never want to come here again!"

"Don't be silly!" she said. "How could that make any difference? It's not important."

He looked up at her, puzzled. "But . . . you must sometimes wonder about him?" he asked.

She shook her head. "Mum's told me all about him," she said, "but I don't even remember his name, I'd have to look it up. He doesn't mean anything to me."

He still seemed unable to understand.

"I think at one time when I was about nine or ten, I used to think he'd turn up in a big car, with lots of presents, and take me out," she admitted. "But I never believed it, even then. I've never thought about it since."

He gazed at her, his eyes full of concern. "What did the children at school say to you?" he asked.

"There was one girl who used to taunt me. She'd say things like 'Where's your father?' But it didn't last long. Mum said that she'd chosen to have me and keep me and this girl's mum had had no choice."

"I wish I could do something for you!" the old man said, with great feeling. He looked as though he yearned to make up for all that she had missed, though she did not think that she had missed anything.

"It's all right!" she said, laughing. "I'm really not bothered!"

At the end of an afternoon's sorting he gave a sigh of satisfaction. "I'm having a busy time!" he stated, not in complaint, but in the tone of someohe who leads a full and active life. "We've got through some work today!"

With visits to the hospital and arranging his affairs, as well as looking after himself, he had plenty to occupy him. But the visits were a great physical effort, and he seemed to tire as the summer progressed. He looked very gaunt sometimes.

Another afternoon he was reading a group of letters which seemed to bring back disquieting memories. He frowned heavily, and pressed his lips together. He did not speak for a long time, and Fran carried on searching and sorting. She found an auctioneer's map from the estate sale at the turn of the century. It had split down the folds when she opened it out, but she could trace all the buildings and fields, the footpath and the coastline, even the seal cave. The lettering was in red and black, in a fine, cursive script. She sellotaped the pieces together again, and did not interrupt the old man in his thoughts.

"I don't like the way your mother calls me an old rogue," he said, when he spoke at last.

"Why not?" asked Fran.

"To us Cornish, a rogue is a liar and a thief," he said. "And I've never been dishonest."

Fran wondered what he had been reading to upset him. "She doesn't mean it like that," she said. "She means someone who knows how to look after himself, someone who can survive. It's something that she admires."

"I've done some bad things in my time, but I've always done what I thought was right."

"Who are your letters from?"

"They're from my daughter, Loveday. She got in with a bad crowd, but I tried to do my best for her. When she married Rowe, I set them up in business. I don't know how they could have failed, any fool could have made a success of it!"

His eyes flashed angrily, and Fran could hear echoes of the roaring family battles that must have taken place. But he was trying to keep calm.

"I bailed them out of that and bought them a house, and Rowe got a labouring job. These are all begging letters. Rowe had been laid off, and there was no money to give Desmond a decent Christmas. Rowe was sick, and Desmond needed clothes for school. And so it went on."

"You did all you could to help," said Fran. "You needn't reproach yourself."

"I thought I did what was right," he said, straining hard to be honest. "But I did it without any charity in my heart. If I could live my life over again, I should try to be more"—he searched for the word—"more gentle."

"Then you wouldn't have lived to be ninety," said Fran.

"Perhaps not," he said, with a return of humour. "But that's not the only thing that matters. I've been too hard in my life, I reckon."

When the last drawer had been tidied, and the contents had all been sorted into tins or were held together in bundles by rubber bands, Mr Treloar seemed sorry that it was finished.

"You'll still come and see me?" he asked anxiously.

"Of course I will," said Fran. "We've got to do some recording."

He must have given it a lot of thought before her next visit. As soon as she arrived he wanted to know if she had brought the recorder. He wanted to wipe out the stories he had already taped, and make a completely fresh start. He knew exactly what he wanted to say, and could hardly wait to begin.

He cleared his throat, and switched on the microphone. "Recollections of a boyhood spent on the Cornish coast around the turn of the century," he announced.

He switched off and looked at Fran, rather pleased with himself but waiting for her approval. She nodded for him to go on.

He began with Penhallow farm and his family, his

parents and his grandparents. The stories flowed without any hesitation, memories of his childhood, the seasons on the farm and the ships that were wrecked on the coast. Every story seemed to lead into the next, in the right order; nothing was out of place.

"It's very good," said Fran, as they finished another tape. "You're putting everything into it."

He looked her in the eyes.

"I reckon I'm putting my very soul into it," he said.

At every visit he began again where he had left off, with no break in the continuity, and throughout the rest of the summer holidays they continued to record the memories of his youth. Her visits during this long spell of hot weather, when day succeeded day, sunny and bright, settled into a pattern; they always did some recording, and very often he had found another box in the back of a cupboard and they could do a bit more 'searching'. Then they played a few games of Fox and Geese, or sometimes draughts or dominoes, and it was time to go.

"Your mother always gives me a kiss when she goes," he said at the end of one afternoon.

"She kisses all her old men," said Fran.

"Couldn't *you* give me a kiss?"

"All right."

She leaned over him and kissed his forehead.

She was disappointed with her examination results. Although she had done extremely well in some subjects, she had done very badly in maths and would have to take it again. She went back to the sixth form, knowing that she would not have a year without exams.

David was now in the second-year sixth. She had not seen him during the holidays, and he suggested going again to the seal cave to look for the set of Fox and Geese. He was keen to find them; it was the old wrecking or beachcombing spirit coming out in him.

131

They went one Saturday afternoon late in September. This time they left the motor-bike where the path joined the road, and walked down the valley. The long dry summer had not yet broken, but the leaves were beginning to turn colour on the trees, and a few had fallen. By the side of the path the brambles were covered with blackberries; occasionally a bright red leaf shone amongst the others. The hawthorn berries were turning red, and old man's beard trailed in the hedgerows.

Where the valley opened out towards the sea, the slopes were covered with heather. It glowed beneath the dried summer grasses, like a slow fire advancing in waves up the hillsides. The lower part of the valley changed very little with the seasons; the bluish rocks, the mine tips, the chimneys of the engine houses were always the same and only the light was different.

They had to wait a while for the tide to go out, and then they splashed through a receding wave to the mouth of the cave. They passed through the tunnels they had been in before, past the shaft to the surface. They marked the wall with an arrow whenever they came to a junction, so that they could find their way back.

It began to smell musty, and the walls glistened with damp. Their breath steamed in the light from their torches. The tunnel was cut out of solid rock, so there were no wooden supports, no beams where a piece of oilcloth could be hidden.

They came to a crumbling, blue-grey rock, and there were pit props to hold up the roof. The wood was soft and mushroomy, and they wondered if it was safe to proceed. They went on cautiously, hardly daring to breathe, and then came to a rock fall which completely blocked the tunnel. The pit props had rotted and given way. One was lying across the passage, and as Fran put her foot on it the bark tore away and the wood squelched under her heel. It was pink in colour, soft and soaking wet.

Dave had a geological hammer, and was tapping the walls. "It's a bit dodgy," he said, his voice sounding strange in the blocked tunnel.

She felt as though the roof might give way above her head. He started to ease stones out of the top of the fall, while she held the light and shone it into the recess, to try to see how far it had caved in. But as he cleared a space, other stones and debris dropped into it. A small avalanche of stones came rolling down the face, with a cloud of dust rising in the torchlight. They moved back for safety.

"It's massive!" said Dave. "It goes back a long way."

The carved wooden pieces, the fox and the two dozen geese in their oilcloth wrapping, were somewhere beyond. The roof of the tunnel had collapsed, burying them behind the stones. They would remain undisturbed now for ever.

They went back to the entrance of the cave, following the marks they had made on the walls. They sat on a flat rock, looking out to sea, where the Atlantic rollers smashed on the reefs and boulders. The noise was loud around them. He reached out his arm and pulled her against him. She put her arm around his waist. He looked into her eyes, and a tear welled up in each one; they slowly trickled down her cheeks.

"What's the matter?" he asked.

"I don't know," she said. It was too complicated to explain.

He felt awkward. After a while he withdrew his arm, and then they moved off across the beach.

Mr Treloar was in great form the next time she saw him. He was very interested in the roof fall; he said the rock she described was what they called 'peachy'. If you were prospecting and you came to this, you knew there was tin not far away. It was 'turning country'. He longed to get down there and have a look at it.

She had only to mention the tunnels of the mine to bring a flood of stories. "Did I tell you about the old woman who was sitting milking her cow in a field?" he asked. "Well, she was sitting on this little three-legged stool, and suddenly the stones of the hedge started falling away. She had the fright of her life, for out popped a head wearing a miner's hat with a lighted candle stuck in a lump of clay on the brim. He gazed around like a mole come out of the ground. She thought it was the devil, and ran screaming back to the farm."

Fran still tried to see him twice a week, once in the evening and once during the weekend. But now that she was in the sixth form, her life seemed to be widening out. There was a sixth-form society and various other activities after school. One weekend she went to a film study conference for students. It took place in a hotel some distance away. They went in the school minibus, leaving after the last lesson on Friday afternoon and staying until tea-time on Sunday. All the summer guests had gone, and the hotel was taken over by groups from schools and colleges, about forty people altogether.

Fran had never stayed in a hotel before, she had never shared a room with other teenage girls. She found it all very strange and new. They watched western films, which she had never thought of taking seriously—they were the sort of films that Nancy watched on television when she was worn out—and had talks about them from university lecturers, and divided into seminars to discuss them.

She found herself separated from David, in a group from other schools. She was fascinated by them, and a little scared at first. They had all seen so many films and read so much, they had so many ideas and expressed them so fluently, she felt that she did not know anything.

At night the images from the films passed through her mind, and she went over and over again the discussion about them. She did not sleep at all the first night, and only fitfully the second, and yet she did not feel tired.

She had told Mr Treloar that she would be away, and then there was work that she would normally have done over the weekend to catch up with, and she did not go to the farm until the following Thursday.

Nancy dropped her at the top of the lane. It was still light, but the evenings were closing in. The sycamore leaves had turned yellow and brown, and had black splotches on them. They were falling from the trees, and she kicked through them on the path. Overhead, a flock of gulls was returning to the coast.

There was no light in the kitchen window, but the door was open and she went in. The kitchen in the evening was very dark; she could just make out the old man sitting hunched in his chair by the fire. She called to him, but he did not stir. She switched on the light.

He jerked awake. "Oh," he sighed. "It's been a long time."

"It's only a week," she said.

"It seemed like years."

"Well, it's not," said Fran. "I told you I couldn't come at the weekend. I've come as soon as I could."

He looked down, pouting with his lips.

"I can't always come to see you twice a week," she said. She did not want to be committed to anything definite. It made her feel trapped if he became upset when she did not see him. "I've got a lot of other things to do."

When he looked up, she saw in the electric light that there were tears in his eyes. Immediately she felt that she had spoken too sharply. She knew how long a week could seem to him, sitting on his own in the house, with only an occasional visitor. He had no television, and rarely listened to the radio. He had only his thoughts, and with nothing but those, a week really could seem like a year.

"I'm sorry," she said, pulling up a chair close to his and taking his hand.

"I've no right to expect you to give up your time," he said. "You've got your own life to lead, and you must do all the things you want to do. You mustn't think about me. But oh! it *did* seem a long time!"

A patient died in the men's ward of the old people's home, and a bed became vacant. There was the possibility of Mr Treloar taking it, though he was quite definite that he did not want to go.

"You must think about it carefully," said Nancy. "You'd be with Lettie."

"I could go on seeing her like I do."

"It's all right at the moment," she said. "But what will you do when the weather gets worse? You find it hard enough getting up to the car as it is."

"I shall manage."

"It'll be your last chance," warned Nancy. "Because if you turn it down this time, they won't offer it to you again."

"If I went into that old people's home," he said with sudden feeling, "I shouldn't last a week. There's nobody there you could have an intelligent conversation with."

And Nancy thought he was right, all the old men there were quite gaga. He would not fit in, and she did not pursue the matter. There were others, anyway, who needed the bed more than he did; only the fact that his wife was already in the home gave him a strong recommendation.

Mrs Treloar continued much the same. She ate well and remained calm, though her clarity of mind varied. Nancy always asked when she left her if she had a message for Tom, and sometimes she said, "Who's Tom?" and at other times she would say, "Tell him, wouldn't it be nice to go around the countryside again, like we used to. Tell him to get me out of here."

He had to cut his visits down to once a week, when the fine autumn weather changed to days of rain. The wind took the last of the leaves from the trees, and the rain turned them to a soggy pulp underfoot. It was too much for him to struggle up the lane in a storm, and he missed some weeks completely.

He celebrated his ninetieth birthday. Fran bought him a birthday card and a book of old mining photographs, and Lettie sent him two cards, one written for her by Nancy and the other written by the nurses at the home. Fran also made him a cake; although she was not very keen on cooking, and did not think she was any good at it, she tried her hand from time to time. It turned out quite well, a Victoria sponge in which she put a filling of cream and jam.

She and Nancy took it to the farm in the evening. The Rowes were already there, sitting in a semi-circle opposite him. They were drinking sherry, and Desmond poured two more glasses. Fran cut the cake.

Mr Treloar had a small slice, and was full of praise for it. She was sure he was doing it mischievously, because his relatives were there, and she found it embarrassing, with Shirley staring at her with barely-concealed hostility.

There was a silence while everyone ate the sponge, which was rather difficult to handle. It was interrupted as the old man spoke.

"Well," he said, making sure that he was being listened to, "I saw my lawyer again this morning."

Any mention of law and wills was like an electrode applied to Desmond. He twitched into life.

"I thought you arranged all that in hospital, Grandad," said Mrs Rowe.

"That was Lettie's will," he said. "Now I've sorted out my affairs."

"Have you altered anything?" asked Vera Rowe cautiously.

Mr Treloar did not hear. "We had some trouble finding the witnesses, I can tell 'ee," he said. "I never see anyone down here except Nurse and her maid, and I couldn't ask them."

"Why not?" asked Vera innocently.

He looked triumphant, as though she had played right into his hands. "Ah well," he said, explaining very carefully. "The witnesses have got to be people not named in the will."

He paused for his words to sink in, observing their effect upon the Rowes. Then he continued, "Yes, it's all settled and my mind's at rest. I've had a marvellous year, a marvellous ninetieth birthday."

He took another bite at the Victoria sponge.

The main work of recording had really been finished, but they still continued, almost out of habit. He had a few afterthoughts to add.

Suddenly he stopped in the middle of a sentence. She glanced up at him, and saw that he looked ill. His face had turned grey, and his eyes were unfocused. His head was swaying. She rushed to him and held him by the shoulders.

"Mr Treloar!" she called. "Tom!"

He seemed to come to, and raised a hand to his forehead. "I think I'm going," he said.

"You're feeling faint," said Fran. She was alarmed, but knew that Tom was always rather melodramatic. She was sure, too, that her mother would think that anyone who could say he was dying probably was not.

"Everything's swimming around."

"I'll get you some brandy," said Fran. He was able to sit up now without support, and she fetched the bottle and poured some into a glass. She held it to his lips. He was no longer staring unseeing ahead of him.

"Shall I phone the doctor?" she asked.

"No!" he said, with returning vigour. "Definitely not!"

"Then I'll phone my mother." He had to be got to bed; he could not do it on his own and he would not want her to help him. She rang Nancy.

She went back and sat by the old man's side. The colour had come back a little into his face, though he still seemed to be shocked. When Nancy arrived, they helped him into the bedroom, and soon he was tucked comfortably under the bedclothes.

"I hope I didn't frighten the maid," he said.

Fran shook her head.

"I didn't want to die when she was here."

"You aren't dying," said Nancy. "You've got nine lives!"

"Well, I reckon I've used up a few of them by now!"

They left the light on in the bedroom, and locked the back door with the spare key, leaving it under a slate on the window-sill. It was a cold, foggy night, and it seemed terrible to leave him there, on his own. Fran thought of him lying in bed in the old sitting-room, the dim light bulb hanging from the beam above, and the long night stretching before him.

"His leg is very swollen again," said Nancy. "It's so heavy, he couldn't lift it on to the bed. I'll ask the doctor to have a look at it tomorrow. And I'll get a bed-cradle for him, to keep the clothes off it. It's burning hot, it must be very painful."

"What would happen if it just goes on swelling?"

"It reaches a point where it bursts, and the water flows out. It seems much easier then, but of course it's cured nothing."

Fran winced; she could feel what it would be like, the

pressure from within on your leg until the water forced a way out. It seemed a worse torture than anything man could devise.

"What happens if he has to stay in bed?" she asked.

"He'd have to go into hospital," said Nancy. "He's got to keep on his feet if he wants to stay at home."

The next morning Nancy was up early, and ready to leave before Fran had finished her breakfast. "Why are you in such a hurry?" Fran asked.

"I want to get down to the farm," said Nancy. "I've had this feeling all night that I should have got the doctor out to Mr Treloar. It'll be awful if I go in and find him dead this morning."

"Do you think he might be?" asked Fran, suddenly fearful.

"Not really," said Nancy. "But I don't feel happy about him."

Fran could not finish her breakfast, and during the day at school she was wondering if the old man was all right. When she reached home, she could not settle to anything. It happened to be one of the evenings when Nancy was late back.

"How is he?" she asked, as soon as her mother came in. She expected the worst after a day of waiting.

"Mr Treloar?" asked Nancy. "When I got there he was cooking bacon and eggs! He said he'd had a marvellous night, though I don't believe him, not with that leg. Anyway, the doctor's been and put him on some new tablets."

Fran felt a surge of relief. He always came through! And yet she knew that one day he would not be able to.

"And he won't have to go to hospital?" she asked.

"He ought to be in bed," said Nancy. "But the doctor says he can stay at Penhallow, as long as he can drag himself about."

★

"That bloody doctor!" exclaimed Nancy, as soon as she came in the next day. "I went in to Mr Treloar this morning and found him nearly dead. It's those new tablets. The doctor told him to take four a day. I checked with the chemist, and he said it's usually one a day, two at the very most.

"They practically killed him. He looked terrible, he was absolutely exhausted. He'd been up all night, he was completely dried out. I couldn't get any pulse on him. And he was supposed to take another four! So I persuaded him to take two. 'Look, you can see how much better your leg is,' I said. And it was true, the swelling had gone right down. 'It might cure my leg,' he said, 'but it's killing *me!*'

"Now, of course, I've got to make it right with Doctor Turner. I can't say to him, 'Look, these tablets are too much for Mr Treloar, he needs to be on half the dose.' Because that will put his back up.

"So I'll have to flounce into the surgery tomorrow and act the little woman. 'Oh Doctor,' I'll say, with a hand on my breast. 'One of my patients, poor old Mr Treloar, is doing badly on his new tablets. What could you possibly suggest?'

"If he's in a good mood he'll laugh and say, 'Cut them down to half.' And if he's in a bad mood because his wife has upset him, then he'll say, 'Tell him to carry on the treatment, I'll see him next week.'

"It makes me mad that we've got to use feminine wiles to get him to do what he ought to do anyway."

"You shouldn't do it," said Fran. "You encourage him to be like that, by accepting it."

"And then the patient would suffer," said Nancy. "I'll accept anything to avoid that."

For a while Nancy made an evening visit—a B.D. visit as she called it—to put Mr Treloar to bed. The doctor had insisted on keeping to the treatment of four tablets a day, but Nancy could not persuade Tom to take more than two, which left him very weak, but with the swelling disappearing from his leg.

Now that the evenings were dark, she was glad of Fran's company for the walk down the lane, with the bare branches rattling in the wind and the fallen leaves slippery underfoot. It reminded them of the first time that they had gone together to Penhallow Farm.

They usually sat and talked for a while before helping the old man to bed.

"There's something I want to ask you," he said one evening as they were sitting round the stove. "Do you believe in an after-life?"

"I don't know," said Nancy.

"I always went to chapel, and listened to what the minister said, but I don't reckon he really knew. You must have seen many people die."

"Yes."

"Well, what I want to know is, have you ever seen any sign that they were going on to another life?"

"I remember one old man, but I don't know if I ought to tell you this," said Nancy. "He was an old miner, he could have given you a few years, and now he was dying. I made him nice and tidy in his bed. He was wearing a shirt, he'd never worn pyjamas in his life. He had a tiny bald head, just like a shrivelled apple. 'Do you want your cap back on?' I asked him. 'I believe I do,' he said. So there he lay, with the bedclothes pulled up to his nose, and two big blue eyes peering over the top, and this great floppy cloth cap on his head. Then all his relatives came in and stood in a semi-circle at the foot of the bed, very solemn. The old man looked at his relatives, then he looked at me, and he said, 'I'd rather be in bed with her than with a policeman'."

Mr Treloar roared with laughter. The noise must have

sounded through the house and echoed down the dark and empty valley. In his weakness, tears came to his eyes, and he wiped them away.

"They were his last words," said Nancy.

"Your mother never takes anything seriously," he said to Fran. "She always turns everything to a joke." The chuckles welled up again, making it impossible for him to speak. Then when he had calmed down, he went on, "But you haven't answered my question. You've always told me the truth. You told me the truth about Lettie when everyone else was saying how well she was. I know I can believe you."

"I don't know the truth," said Nancy. "Nobody does."

"But what do you think?"

"I think it's an end," said Nancy. "I've never had any feeling that the person was going to another life."

"That's what I thought."

"But that's only my opinion," added Nancy. "Shall I ask the minister to call?"

"No you won't!" he said emphatically.

They put him to bed, and when he was tucked under the eiderdown, with his leg beneath the hump of the cradle, Nancy said, "I saw Lettie this afternoon. I asked her if she had a message for you, and she said, 'Tell him to keep warm.'"

"I'm glad to cool off a bit," he said. "When my leg was hot it was like being in bed with a warming pan!"

"Have you got a message for Lettie?"

"Tell her I'll come and see her again, as soon as I get off these damn tablets. They're such terrible things. If you see Doctor Turner, you can give *him* a message. You can tell him those tablets he gave me, they'd get water out of granite!"

Fran always felt a sort of horror at leaving him alone, in an isolated farmhouse at the end of a rough farmtrack, with only the telephone to connect him with the outside world. And if he needed to phone, he would probably not be able to reach it. She knew what she would like to do.

"Mum," she said cautiously. "If Mr Treloar gets worse, and can't stay any longer on his own at the farm, do you think we could have him here?"

"No," said Nancy, taken by surprise but in no doubt at all as to her reaction.

"Why not?"

"We're not a nursing home."

"It would be the best solution."

"It's out of the question," said Nancy. "You can't take in everyone who needs to be looked after. I've got one old man at the moment who lives in a caravan with a leaking roof. He sits there all day with plastic bags tied on his feet and a plastic sack over his lap. It would be the best solution for him as well."

"I'd *like* Mr Treloar to come here," said Fran. She had thought it all out. "I'd look after him. It wouldn't make any extra work for you."

"I couldn't have anyone here, it would be unprofessional," said Nancy. "It would be unfair to the other patients." Now that she had had time to think about it, she saw more and more objections. "And have you thought about what it means? It would be taking on an enormous responsibility. You'd be committed to it, you'd never be able to have a holiday, you'd never be able to go away even for a day. He'd always be there to be looked after until he died."

"I know."

"It's the sort of commitment that most families are trying to avoid. We couldn't do it!" She reached out a hand to Fran's shoulder. "It's very kind, but it wouldn't work, love. And think what the relatives would say! They'd be convinced we were only doing it for his money."

"I don't care what they think."

"Look," said Nancy, trying to consider it for Fran's sake. "If he was so bad that he couldn't be left on his own at the farm, he couldn't be left on his own here all day. It would be no different."

"I could stay home . . ."

"Oh no!" said Nancy decisively. "You've got your schoolwork."

Fran realised—as she had always really known—that it was impossible. Yet it was the first time in her life that she had felt very strongly that she knew what she wanted. It even seemed to her an odd thing to want, and yet she was quite certain.

"He may be all right," said Nancy. Then she laughed. "And you can always look after me when I get old!"

For day after day the weather continued misty and cold. Fran re-sat her maths exam, and started rehearsals for the school Christmas pantomime, in which she and David both had (as Dave said) small parts—walking on their knees as two of the dwarfs in Snow White.

She still saw Mr Treloar regularly. He was now on one tablet a day, which seemed to suit him fine; Nancy stopped her B.D. visits and Fran forgot her wish to bring him home, because it seemed as though he could go on at Penhallow for a long time.

One evening Fran was in the house on her own when the phone rang. It was Sister Williams at the old people's home, and Fran gave her the number that Nancy had left if anyone wanted to get in touch with her.

"Is it about Mrs Treloar?" she asked.

"Yes, I thought I'd let your mother know so that she could prepare the old man," said the nurse. "She's very poorly. I don't know, but I've got a feeling that she may go during the night."

Fran wondered whether her mother would want Mr

Treloar to visit his wife, or whether she would think it was too much effort for the old man, and not want to disturb him.

She felt sure that he would wish to be with Lettie. As she sat on her own, she imagined the unexpectedly late call at the farm, and Tom turning out into the night, in his overcoat and cloth cap, the lights of torches flashing in the dark wet lane and shining on the metal of his pulpit as he struggled upwards through the wind and the rain, on one of the last significant journeys of his life.

She had already gone to bed when Nancy came home, but was still awake; she called her mother into her room. Nancy said that she had phoned the Rowes and they had met at the farm to fetch the old man. When she saw Mrs Treloar she did not think she would die that night.

"She's very poorly though. She's very weak, she was yawning heavily. 'Look how tired she is!' said Vera, but that wasn't tiredness, it was lack of oxygen. She was very dehydrated, I gave her a cup of water and she drank it all. She was quite conscious. Tom sat by the side of the bed and talked to her. 'Don't leave me, Lettie!' he said. 'We've been together all these years!' She kept slipping into unconsciousness, but she knew him all right. Then he wanted to kiss her, but he couldn't lean forward far enough, so we tried to lift her up to him, Sister Williams on one side and me on the other. And we couldn't manage it!"

Nancy bit her lip. "It was awful really. There we were, struggling to get her up, and she was wondering what we were trying to do to her. We gave up in the end.

"Then Mr Treloar says to Sister Williams, in his great booming voice, 'You needn't worry, nurse—I've made all the arrangements for the funeral.' 'I want another drink,' pipes up Mrs Treloar. So I got her a drink and sister attached the undertaker's card to her notes.

"Vera went on about why did they leave her like this,

why wasn't a doctor there? I had to ask her to keep quiet. Desmond didn't say a word.

"Mr Treloar got up to go, and I helped him along. Then he stopped, rested on his frame, and turned and looked back at Lettie. 'I'll never see her no more,' he said."

Fran thought that one of the Rowes might have stayed with him that night, but nobody did. Nancy rang the old people's home the next morning, and Lettie was much the same. When she went to see Mr Treloar at midday, he was sitting in front of a plate of pork and beans which the home help had cooked.

"I must eat this, because I've got to be strong," she heard him saying aloud to himself as she came in. "I shall have a lot to do this week."

He expected to hear that Lettie had died, and had been waiting for the phone to ring all morning. Nancy told him that it might take several days. Lettie was in no pain, she was just dying of old age.

He wondered if he ought to go and see her again, but Nancy did not think it was necessary, unless he really wanted to.

"I don't think so," he said. "I've said goodbye to her."

When Nancy saw her she was looking very gaunt, with hollow eyes and her cheeks drawn in. Sister Thomas was back on duty, and she had her sitting up and was trying to get her to eat. "I'm going to keep her alive," she said, spooning custard between her lips. "It's a challenge!" Nancy thought it would be kinder to let her go.

When Sister Williams came back she showed Nancy the old lady's sores. There were blisters on her back and heels, and she bruised if they touched her. If she had been any more conscious, she would have been very uncomfortable.

The next time Nancy visited the old people's home

Sister Thomas came rushing up to her, anxious for her not to see Mrs Treloar.

"We're just attending to her. If you could come back another time . . ."

"Of course!" said Nancy. "I quite understand."

She knew that Sister Thomas did not want her to see the old lady's blisters, not knowing that Nancy had seen them already. When she went back Mrs Treloar looked little different; her skin was now almost transparent, like old paper. She was fading away, very slowly.

The phone call came exactly at eight o'clock. Fran turned down the transistor on the breakfast table while Nancy answered it. Mrs Treloar had died during the night. They wanted to know whether they should inform Mr Treloar.

"No," said Nancy. "I'll go and tell him."

So while Fran sat on the school bus, looking out at the grey winter landscape, the bare trees and the mist-covered fields, she imagined her mother letting herself into the farmhouse kitchen and telling the old man as he sat in his wooden chair by the stove. It would be what he expected, yet even so it would still be a shock, after being together for over sixty years. It was longer than Fran could imagine.

She felt that somehow he would look different, after the loss of a lifetime's partner. But he looked just the same, in his usual chair beneath the cream-painted mantelshelf and the brown and white china dog. The grey rug over his knees trailed on the floor, and a red glow spread from the bottom of the stove. She put her bag with the tape-recorder and library books on the table. They were both thinking about Lettie.

"I'm sorry," she said.

"I'm glad she went first," he said. "I wouldn't like her to be left without anyone to care about her."

He had gone to the funeral. Fran had wondered if she and her mother would go, but Nancy never went to patients' funerals. She said, too, that the custom amongst the old people was for the men to go to the funeral, while the women stayed at home.

Although she had brought the recorder, she did not take it out; it did not seem appropriate. She sat down in the chair at the other side of the fire. They were silent for a while.

"I've left the farm to Desmond," he said suddenly.

"Yes," she said. She had always supposed that it would be his, once Cousin Win had departed.

"I wanted to leave it to you," he went on, looking across at her.

"To me?" she asked, startled.

"I'd rather you have it than Desmond. I debated it for a long time, and in the end I thought family had to come first, I don't know why. But I'd like it to go to you, there's still time to change my will . . ."

"Oh no, you mustn't!" said Fran. She had a feeling of panic, of trouble coming. She could see clearly the fuss that it would create. The Rowes would be frantic; they would fight it in the courts.

And at the same time she had a growing feeling that the farmhouse, its garden and its outbuildings, could be hers! The fields and the wood and the marshy pond, the whole valley down to the sea, it could all be hers!

She was astonished at the strength of this desire for possession. It was greed; she had no right to any of it.

"He'll only put it up for sale," said Mr Treloar. "He's got no feeling for it."

The whole of the old man's life had been put into Penhallow, and his father's and his grandfather's lives; no one could own it as they had done. There was no one who could have the same right to it.

"If only I'd had a son, or a grandson who wanted to

149

farm!" he said. Then he looked closely at her. "What would you do with it?"

She could open a guesthouse, she could run it as a pony-trekking stables; fantasies such as these came rapidly to mind. They all diminished the place.

She shook her head. "You mustn't, it wouldn't be right."

"Why must I leave it to someone who hates me?"

"Because he's your family," she said.

The next time she saw him he seemed very agitated. "Where's St Kitts?" he asked as soon as she entered the room.

"It's an island," said Fran.

"But where is it?" he repeated. "I've got to know!"

"All right," she said calmly. "I'll look it up."

She fetched his atlas, in which a third of the world was coloured the bright red of the British Empire. She found that it was in the West Indies, and placed the open book on his lap. He took it as though he could not wait to see, and his finger trembled as he pointed to the spot.

Still very tense, he began to record. He told how very early one morning he had gone down to the beach with his gun. The mist hung over the sea and the cliffs. Suddenly amongst the rocks of the shore he found himself face to face with a young black boy. They were both startled, and stood staring at each other for several minutes. Then they spoke. The boy had sailed from St Kitts and had jumped ship when it came to Hayle. He was walking along the coast until he reached another port. After a while they went their separate ways into the mist.

He stopped. "I should dearly love a cup of tea," he said.

It was unusual for him to want a drink; he neither ate

nor drank anything after midday, except for a cup of milk at five o'clock, and he always kept to his routine.

"All right," said Fran. "I'll make some tea."

She went out to the scullery. As she waited for the kettle to boil she thought of the encounter on the shore of the young Cornishman and the black boy, facing each other across the rocks as the mist swirled in from the sea. It was strange that he had only just remembered it.

She thought she could hear his voice continuing to record in the other room. As she took in the teapot and jug of milk, she heard him saying, "Here comes the maid."

She put the pot under its thatched-cottage tea-cosy on the stove, and fetched the blue and white cups and saucers from the dresser. She poured him a cup, which he sipped and declared first-rate.

"Are you going to do any more recording?" she asked.

"No, I've finished now," he said.

She packed away the recorder, and cleared the tea-things. He had left most of the tea in his cup. She kissed him on the top of the head, and said goodbye.

"I'll see you next week," she added.

But she never saw him again. Three days later she came back from school after a rehearsal for the pantomime, and Nancy said, "I've got some bad news for you."

Fran thought immediately of Mr Treloar.

"He died last night."

It seemed unreal to her at first, like a play. She could not really believe that someone could be there one moment, and then suddenly they were not.

Her mother told her how the home help had gone in as usual that morning, and found him dead in his arm-chair. He must have been sleeping again in his chair by the stove, and had had a heart attack during the night. He was curled up, his head on one side. He had not tried to reach the phone.

"He was all right when I saw him," said Fran. "He did some recording, he seemed so well."

"It could have happened at any time."

"But Lettie seemed to go on and on. I thought . . . I didn't think it would be so sudden."

"It's as he would have wished," said Nancy. "That's how he wanted to go."

"At least he died in his own home," said Fran. She felt relieved about that; he had not had to go into a private nursing home, or be taken off into a hospital ward. He had stayed at Penhallow.

But she could not feel that he had gone, even if she knew it to be true.

On the day of the funeral she went to school as normal, but she could not stop thinking about the afternoon. At the end of the morning's lessons, Dave took her home on the back of his motor-bike. It was a cold, bleak day, with showers of rain driven by the wind. She was freezing after the ride, and could not stop shivering. Her mother made her a hot drink.

Nancy had taken it for granted that they would go to the funeral, and she said nothing about it being a family occasion, or the local tradition that the women stayed at home. It was to take place at the Methodist chapel at two o'clock, and they did not want to arrive early. They had a long wait, and the time passed slowly.

Eventually Nancy, who had changed out of her uniform, said, "Right, shall we be off then?" and they drove down the long village street to the chapel.

The hearse was standing outside, the back door open, the coffin surrounded with flowers. A few people were watching from the other side of the road. Fran and her mother hurried into the chapel, out of the icy wind, and slipped into an empty pew at the back.

It was dark inside, the winter afternoon light barely

penetrating the tall windows. It was strange to be there. At one time she used to go to Sunday School with some of her junior school friends, but she had never been since. She felt very little emotion, only strangeness. She had thought that she would feel sad, but she did not feel at all like crying. She looked around her.

They were all men in the pews opposite. "You see the fat man in the front," whispered Nancy. "That's Frank Pascoe!"

Fran looked at her mother and they smiled, both knowing how mad Mr Treloar would have been that Frank Pascoe was there at his funeral.

Then Nancy nudged her and they stood up, and the men opposite slowly rose to their feet as well. The coffin was being brought in to the chapel and taken up the aisle on a sort of trolley, between four men in black suits. It was followed by Desmond and Vera Rowe and other members of the family, cousins and great-nephews and nieces whom she did not recognise, though there was no Cousin Win. She felt Shirley passing close by her, but they avoided looking at each other. The procession moved slowly forward, and then the bearers sat behind Frank Pascoe, and the family took the front two pews on the side where Fran and her mother were sitting. The coffin was on its own in the centre.

She heard the words that the minister was saying only as sounds, not making any sense of them. She looked at the coffin, beneath a wreath of chrysanthemums. She could think only that Tom Treloar lay there; she could think of nothing else.

Suddenly Nancy was tugging her sleeve, and everyone was kneeling down to pray. She knelt, but could not pray with the words of the minister.

Then it was over, and the coffin and family were coming back down the aisle. Shirley had tears in her eyes; she looked at Fran and smiled.

They went by car to the cemetery. The coffin was carried along the path, followed by the mourners. Under the grey sky and in the drizzling rain, the procession of dark–clothed figures passed between the gravestones towards a hedge of windswept trees.

They stopped on the narrow path beneath the hedge, by the side of the open grave. It was where Lettie had been buried only a week ago. Fran felt that she could not look, and yet she wanted to.

The mound of earth was covered with a green cloth of imitation grass. The coffin rested across two ropes, and was lowered into the grave. As it slid out of sight, she clutched her mother's hand, and Nancy squeezed her hand in return.

"Ashes to ashes, dust to dust . . ."

She had heard the words before, and the minister spoke them in a mechanical sort of way, and yet she had never imagined that they could mean so much. The tears flowed down her face as the earth rattled against the coffin.

The mourners passed in slow procession along the foot of the grave. She stood for a moment looking down at the coffin in the wet earth.

All the flowers were rustling in the wind and the rain.

A day or two later Nancy went to Penhallow to collect the frame. She walked down with Mr Laity, from the farm on the top road, and when they entered she thought the house had been burgled. "It looked as though a bomb had hit it!" she told Fran. Drawers were pulled out, cupboards left open, and the contents strewn all over the place. There were the remains of a bonfire in the yard.

Mr Laity said that he had seen the red car go down the lane several times, so Nancy assumed that the Rowes had been there. She picked up the frame, and left.

"What were they doing?" asked Fran.

"They were probably looking for the will," said Nancy.

"But why did they pull everything out?"

"I expect they took what they wanted, before any of the other relatives could get there. And he hasn't been dead a week!"

Fran thought of all the searching she had done with him; and now she would never go there again.

The pantomime was finished, all the activities and parties of the end of term were over, and the holidays had begun. In the post one morning, amongst the Christmas mail, were two identical envelopes, franked in red with the name of a firm of solicitors. She opened the one addressed to her, and read that Mr Thomas Treloar, deceased, had left her the sum of one hundred pounds, which would be forwarded to her when the estate was settled. All she could really notice was the word 'deceased'; it seemed to make his death official. There was a further note to say that Mr Laity, of Higher Penhallow, was holding a package for her, which she should collect.

Nancy had a similar letter. "I shall give the money to the nurses' fund," she said.

"You won't," said Fran. "That's not what he wanted."

"I'll think about it," said Nancy, and she went off to work.

Fran cycled to Mr Laity's farm, along the bare lanes through the misty countryside. The 'package' was much larger than she expected; it was a cardboard box full of the photograph albums, letters and postcards that she had tidied. She would have to ask her mother to collect it.

But inside was a smaller parcel, wrapped in brown paper and sealed. She took it home and opened it. There, lying in tissue, were the two pieces of jewellery that had belonged to Mr Treloar's mother, the amber necklace and her gold wedding ring. She took them out, and held the amber up to the light.

155

She understood why they had been left with Mr Laity. The old man had known what would happen after his death, and had taken this precaution in case they simply disappeared. She thought of him playing Fox and Geese; no one would outwit him over a will. She smiled to think that he never lost his cunning.

She placed the recorder on the kitchen table, amongst the wrappings and the tissue paper. She had not yet listened to the tape they had made on her last visit. She switched on.

It was strange to hear his voice again, just as when he was alive, and it brought back vividly all the times she had spent with him. It was like living the evening again. She remembered the farmhouse kitchen, the glow from the stove, the chair she was sitting in; it was as if she was there. The only difference was that now she knew it was the last time.

She heard again the story of his encounter with the boy on the shore, that misty day at the beginning of the century.

His voice stopped, and there were some clicks on the tape. Then she heard her own voice, sounding very distant. "All right," she said. "I'll make some tea." There was a pause, during which she could hear the sound of his breathing above the hum of the machine. Then his voice spoke again, with an immediacy which startled her, as though he had come into the room.

"Right!" he said with great determination. "Now that you're out of the way, I want to put this on record, once and for all." He paused, to make sure that he got it right. "I want you to know how much I appreciate your visits. I look forward to your coming, and it's made all the difference to this last year. You've given me something to live for. Thank you for your kindness, and God bless you!"

There was a long pause, at the end of which he said

hurriedly, "Here comes the—" The tape clicked, and then there was silence.

Fran sat there without stopping the recorder, the hum seeming to continue the time of the other day, his presence still there in the room.

"I did nothing," she thought. "I only went there, rather reluctantly at first. I only listened to him. I didn't do it out of kindness, I enjoyed it. I'd rather have him back than all the legacies."

The tape came to an end, and the machine ejected the cassette.

In the New Year, just before the end of the holidays, she and David walked down the valley again. It was swampy underfoot, and the trees, stunted and lichen-covered, had the appearance of a primeval forest. She stopped at the point where the footpath rose a little up the hillside, and she could see over the grey tops of the trees to the other side of the valley. The farmhouse and its buildings clung to the slope amongst the ash and sycamore and a few pines that Tom had planted himself.

There were no signs of life, no smoke from the chimney; the windows were empty and bare. Dave stood by her side and looked at it with her.

"It's an amazing place," he said. And then he added, joking, "A pity he didn't leave it to you."

"He nearly did," said Fran.

"You didn't play your cards right," he said.

She shook her head. She valued the mementoes that had been left to her, the photographs and letters, and above all the tapes that she had made with all his stories on them.

"But think what you could do with it," said Dave. "You could clear all those woods and put in chalets down to the stream."

She knew that he was teasing.

"You could put caravans in the fields at the top," he went on.

It would be the worst that could happen to Penhallow, but planning restrictions made it unlikely, though not impossible. Desmond had already put it up for auction, and she was afraid that it might be bought by a development company.

She would like to see a young Cornishman buying it to farm, but no one like that could possibly afford it. It would most likely be bought as a holiday home by rich people from out of the county.

It would never again be like the farm where Thomas Treloar was born and lived his life and died. But even if it belonged to her, she could not keep it the same forever.

"Come on!" said David. He took her hand and they walked on through the valley to the sea.